To My BFF

Myrna Ellingson Kurle

You have shared the joy in the good times of my life, and provided light during the dark periods. Thank you for being my best friend during the last forty years.

In Memory of
Jacob 'Jack' Kurle
A Good Man
A Great Father
A Dear Friend
We Miss You

CHAPTER ONE

Lexie sat on the rock wall that kept the ocean at bay. She came because of a promise to a colleague. Sarah Chandler helped her once, and Lexie offered to return the favor. She never expected that the Dallas detective would ever request assistance from a rural sheriff.

The waves curled toward her then bubbled into white foam before dissolving. Sprinkles of water danced around her bare legs and feet. In spite of the visual beauty of Alabama's Sandsun Resort, she longed for home in Diffee, Oklahoma.

A girl vanished—Sarah's niece. Lexie came to find the missing teenager. Her long dark hair, in one braid, was twisted into a knot on her head. Sunglasses shaded her blue eyes. The scar on the right side of her face glistened from sweat. Blue jeans and shirtsleeves were rolled up in an attempt to cool down.

The missing girl's family condo sits on the hill above Lexie. The road winding into the vacation home was visually accessible from Lexie's rock perch. She'll wait for Sarah's vehicle to arrive, then tromp up the incline to meet the grieving family. Lexie was determined to hang back and observe the family dynamics. Sarah gave no indication a family member was involved, but people are often blind to their relative's sins.

A mesmerizing, splashing lullaby played around her. It helped filter out her chagrin at leaving her baby and job to search for a girl way outside her jurisdiction.

MURDER

and

BEYOND

A SHERIFF LEXIE WOLFE NOVEL

BOOK 4, 2nd Edition

DONNA WELCH JONES

Twisted Plot Publishing

This is a work of fiction. Names, characters, places, and incidents are products of the author's imagination or are used fictitiously and are not to be construed as real. Any resemblance to actual events, locales, organizations, or persons, living or dead, is entirely coincidental.

Twisted Plot Publishing
21938 So. Hickory Lane
Tahlequah, Oklahoma, 74464
Published in the Unites States of America

ISBN-13: 978-0-9970148-4-6

Lexie didn't move or look up when she heard footsteps. Others passed this way earlier never interrupting her solitary watch. These footsteps, however, stopped.

Her eyes widened and studied a man whose skin had turned to hide from sun exposure. He was probably in his seventies. He had a stern face, accusing eyes and muscular arms that held a casserole dish.

"You that sheriff they said was coming?" he barked.

Lexie scooted around, then braced a hand against the ground to stand. "Yes, Lexie Wolfe."

His words huffed out, "Police around these parts aren't happy about rich folks bringing in outsiders to butt into their cases."

"The law enforcement is family. Emma's Great Aunt is a detective, and I'm her friend. Your name?"

"Virgil Sullivan."

"Is that yummy smelling food on the way to the Chandler's?"

"My wife cooked it up. She feels bad for the kid's family."

"You seem indifferent, Virgil."

"Rich folks move in for the summer and act like they own the town. They treat us like servants."

Lexie removed her sunglasses. "You think that's why Emma disappeared—someone paid back the rich folks?"

"It wouldn't have happened if they stayed home where they belonged."

His body turned, and his feet tromped away.

She sank back onto the rocky ledge. Ten minutes later another man stopped at her roost. Probably around fifty, but his shoulders curled forward like a much older man. His raccoon eyes searched the horizon.

"The ocean is calm today." His voice blended with the swish of the waves.

Lexie looked up, "It's beautiful."

"It turns into a raging beast that eats humans."

"I'm Lexie Wolfe. Your name?"

"Amos Hicks."

"Do you know Emma Chandler's family?"

"I took her dad out on my fishing boat a few times."

"Have you heard any rumors about where Emma ended up?"

"Some say she took off with the Sullivan boy. Others think her stepmother did her in. Bunch of fools talkin' with no thought of the pain her dad's goin' through."

"You understand his pain?"

"Two of my daughters died."

Lexie gulped, "Are they still investigating?"

"There aren't any criminals to arrest. The ocean took them both. Crystal drowned on Halloween. Hannah walked into the ocean on New Year's Eve."

"Walked in?"

"Hannah left a suicide note. She wrote that the waves beckoned. She apologized for leaving, but she wanted to join her sister."

Lexie reached out a comforting hand. He shook his head no. "Was Crystal's body found?"

"No, but I know the ocean took her. She was at a friend's beach party. She swam out too far and vanished. The current must've pulled her under. The kids were afraid to dive to look for her body after they saw a fin in the vicinity."

"I'm so sorry."

"Too late for my daughters, but I pray the Chandler girl shows up." The man walked away.

Lexie decided that polite farewells were hard to come by in this community.

Amos' hurried steps stopped abruptly. He called back, "There's rumors circulating about sex trafficking in these parts."

Lexie's hand acknowledgement of the information was lost behind his exiting body.

She found a small patch of shade, pulled her cell phone out of her pocket, and punched in her office number. The answering person was her deputy and brother, Tye.

"What's up, Sis? Miss me already? Or maybe you don't trust me to protect the fine people of Diffee in your absence?"

"I'm bored from waiting for Sarah. Time to develop a plan and get this investigation started."

"Learned anything?"

"Two men crossed my path. Virgil resents the rich summer people. Amos shared some town gossip. Is everything okay there?"

"Probably."

"That sounds ominous."

"I received a report that Wendy Elliot didn't come home from school. She was an hour overdue when her mom phoned me in a panic."

"An hour is nothing when it comes to a late teenager," Lexie replied.

"I know, but I tried to pacify, empathize, and sympathize."

"Listen to the waves." Lexie faced her phone toward the ocean.

"Got one better, Sis, listen to this."

The sound of thunder blasted into Lexie's ear. "Are you standing outside?"

"Yep, looks like a light show with all the lightning in the distance. The storm coming is one reason Wendy's mom is upset. Tornado warnings are out and parts of Oklahoma are in for a grisly night. A tornado isn't headed this way—at least not yet. Hopefully, one of the bastards won't turn on us."

Lexie's ears caught the rumple of tires on gravel. "Sarah's finally here. I saw a white SUV go past. I better head to the condo. My priority is to start and end this investigation as soon as possible."

"Later."

"Goodbye," Lexie responded.

CHAPTER TWO

Tye's Case

Deputy Tye Wolfe stood outside the sheriff's office. Foreboding twisted his innards. The humid stickiness in the air brought beads of sweat to his forehead. The wind held its breath—waiting to heave out in swirls of dread and doom. May in Oklahoma was like gambling. With a little luck the funnels on the weatherman's chart won't show up over Diffee. Hopefully, the black clouds mounting all day will collapse into thunderstorms instead of spiraling into tornados.

The hairs standing up on the back of his neck predicted bad to worse for a town somewhere in the state. Perhaps unkind to pray his small town will be spared, but this was his community, his people, so maybe God can forgive his selfishness.

He pulled back his black hair and fastened a Cherokee band. His earthen colored skin and prominent nose belied the fact that his Cherokee father married a white woman. His sister, Lexie, ended up with the blue eyes and fine features of their mother. Tye felt fortunate that his proud heritage was visible on the outside of his person.

He retraced his steps into the office. The space was a conglomeration of four old desks and ten mismatched metal file cabinets in a row. The conference area held a six foot white plastic table with fold-up chairs. Only a bouquet of red roses on Delia's desk and a photo of a rainbow that hung above her three-legged computer table broke up the brown hues of the floor and walls.

"Delia, you head home, and get ready to spend time in the cellar tonight."

The woman at the computer struggled to her feet. "I need a new knee. This left knee gives me fits."

Tye smiled, "You know doctors can replace knees?"

"Lord-a-mercy, I'm in my mid-sixties. If I get a new knee now I'll require a second surgery before I die. I read that they only last fifteen years."

"It might be worth not having the pain, and a hitch in your get-along."

"I'll put the surgery off a few years. If I lost fifty pounds, my knee might recover."

A rumple of thunder activated Delia's momentum. "Oops! I'll lock up these folders."

"Let me," Tye offered. "Go home before the storm hits."

If I don't blow away tonight, I'll see you in the morning."

Delia grabbed her purse, lunch bag, and plastic drink cup then scurried out the door.

Tye watched, through the window, as she swung open her car door. The hem of her plaid dress swirled, and wisps of gray hair protruded from her head. The wind came up in the short time since he was outside."

He punched the button on his ringing cell phone, "Wolfe here."

"Tye, it's Betty Elliot. Wendy hasn't come home. It's goin' be a bad one tonight. I feel the storm in my bones."

"Have you phoned her friends? Talked to the school?"

"My girl doesn't have many friends. I phoned a couple of kids, but they didn't know anything. Principal said Wendy answered morning roll call. He hasn't talked to all her teachers to make sure she stayed all day."

"I'll do some checking," Tye promised. "She probably lost track of time."

"She always phones me—a good girl. The strain in her voice tightened. "Please find her, Tye."

"I'll get on it right now."

Tye pushed the red button, then the green one to call his wife, Jamie. "Hon, are you and the boys ready to hang out in the basement?"

"Seth and Gabriel put toys in their backpacks. Brody and Adam are on the way over. I used mom dramatics to get them to come. They think they're so tough at twenty-two that a tornado will circle them."

"Glad I don't have to worry about them."

"Barbeque ribs are about ready. When are you coming home?"

"I've got to work a little longer. Wendy Elliot didn't come home after school. Her mom is panicking. Is Wendy one of your students? I must figure out if she disappeared during the school day or after."

"She's not in last hour sports with me, but is in my history class. Let me think. She's so quiet I hardly know when she's present. Come to think of it—she wasn't in class. When I asked about her I got shrugs, and a couple of 'who cares.'"

"What hour is she in your class?"

"She's in my second class after lunch."

"Okay, that helps."

"Now I wish I'd followed up." Concern trickled into Jamie's words.

"I'll figure it out. I'll come home as soon as possible."

Tye radioed Lexie's other deputy. "J.J., head back to cover the office. A girl didn't make it home from school. I'll go check the building."

"I'm on my way," J.J. responded.

Tye locked the front door and jogged to the cruiser. He slid onto the seat, and heaved the door shut against the winds resistance.

A sixteen-year-old shouldn't wander around outside in this weather. It's a strange coincidence that Lexie is looking for a teen girl in Alabama while I do the same in Oklahoma.

CHAPTER THREE

Lexie's Case

Lexie made a path up the jagged rocks. Then crossed the manicured lawn that stretched in front of the condo.

Sarah spoke as she pulled a bag out of her rental vehicle. "Been waiting long, Lexie?"

"Admiring the ocean for three hours."

"Sorry, my flight got out late. All you had to do was knock on their door."

"Wanted you with me when I met your family. Anything I should know before we go in?"

Sarah shook her head, "They're regular folks."

"Regular rich people?"

Sarah's eyes caught Lexie's face with a sneer. "What does wealth have to do with it?"

"A local came up to me on the beach. He indicated that people around here resent the rich summer visitors. Perhaps that's the motive for Emma's disappearance."

"So you're already at work," Sarah snorted. "I thought you were enjoying the scenery and getting some sun."

Lexie trailed behind Sarah. Red capris, flowered shirt, and a slouchy hat that covered her bobbed brunette hair made Sarah look like a beach grandma. Lexie, however, knew this woman was no defenseless granny. She was a spitfire with an ace shot. Short, stout, and the excess diameter on Sarah's upper arms was muscle, not fluff. The woman's fifty something years served her well on undercover operations. No criminal even suspected her profession until after she beat the shit out of him.

Sarah's nephew swung the door open before they knocked. A red-blotched face and dark circled eyes revealed his worry and lack of sleep. His short brick-house stature marked he and Sarah as family. The third similar stature in

11

the room belonged to Sarah's great nephew. Tanner, a sullen faced teen, loitered in the corner offering his great aunt no welcome.

Sarah's sharp reprimand disturbed the quiet. "Think you're too grown-up to give your old auntie a hug? Come over here right now."

The teen returned her vivacious hug. A smile started to move his lips, but evaporated into thin air.

"Lexie, this is my nephew; Devon, great nephew; Tanner, and Cass—Devon's new wife.

"I'm not that new, Aunt Sarah." Her tone sounded irritated, not playful, and Cass didn't offer a welcoming touch. Her red lips stretched into a failed smile.

"Everyone on the sofa," Sarah ordered. "Let's figure out what happened to Emma."

The trio sat on a curved leather sofa, a section separated each of them.

Sarah tossed a pen and pad toward Lexie. "Take notes, my brain requires reminders."

Lexie sat on a recliner opposite the family. Her eyes focused to study body language, and ears ready to listen for inflections. The pen in her hand was ready to transcribe.

"Devon, when did you first realize that Emma was missing?" Sarah's voice sounded calm, even.

"I was on a three day business trip. I don't know what happened prior to my arrival."

Cass crossed her legs. "I have no idea about Emma's comings and goings. Anyway, I shopped in New Orleans when Devon was away."

Tanner chimed in, "Emma left with Zane. He picked her up before noon to go snorkeling. That was the last time I saw her."

Devon continued, "I arrived home around 7 p.m. When Emma still wasn't home at ten, I started to phone Zane's folks."

"Why didn't you?" Lexie asked.

"Cass told me for the millionth time that I'm overprotective, and to back off Emma's social life."

Cass glared, "You think her disappearance is my fault?"

Devon shrugged, "I finally phoned Zane at midnight. I tried Emma's phone at least a dozen times before that, but it didn't ring or...."

Sarah interrupted, "You talked to Zane?"

"Yes. He claimed that she wanted to hang out with her girlfriends. He left her in town around 8 p.m."

Lexie leaned forward, "Who were the girls?"

"He didn't know. Dropped her off at the theater then he left. Told me the other girls were already inside."

Sarah's jaw tightened, "Zane ever show signs of violent behavior? Quick temper? Bruises on Emma?"

Cass piped in, "Any bruises on Emma were inflicted by her brother, not Zane. They fight like a couple of rabid dogs."

Tanner's jaw jutted, "You're the only person who hates Emma. Did you hurt her?"

Cass grabbed a book from the glass coffee table and flung it toward her stepson. "You little shit!"

Sarah jumped to her feet. "ENOUGH! We have to find Emma. You three aren't to blame for her disappearance. You're worried and sleep deprived. Stick together instead of falling apart."

Lexie wasn't ready to rule out any of the three. Sarah's assumption that it wasn't their faults was premature. Familial DNA hampered Sarah's judgment.

Sarah eased back into the side chair and continued. "What did you do after you talked to Zane?"

Tanner spoke, "I phoned three girls she hangs out with and asked if she was at the show. They didn't see her that night."

Sarah looked at Devon, "What's law enforcement's take on her disappearance?"

"Chief Swinson said it's too soon to send out the troops. An eighteen-year-old is an adult, so if one decides to take off it's her personal business, and none of his."

Lexie spoke, "Any home problems that might motivate her to leave?"

Devon looked toward Cass. She responded, "Putting it simply, she doesn't like me and never has."

"She's leaving for a college summer course in ten days. There was no reason to run off to get away from us," Tanner added.

Devon paced. "We've called all our relatives. She hasn't showed anywhere."

"Does she have access to cash?" Lexie asked.

"No job—just an allowance she spends as soon as she gets," Devon replied.

Sarah pulled keys from her pocket. "Where can we find this Zane?"

"He works at the scuba shop on the beach," Tanner volunteered. "I'll show you."

Lexie followed Tanner and Sarah out the door. Lexie slid into the backseat— Tanner road shotgun.

"Tanner you're my GPS," Sarah stated.

"After you get to the bottom of the hill take a left, then we'll go straight about four miles before we turn off toward the ocean," Tanner instructed.

Lexie offered no conversation; she only wanted to hear theirs.

"What's this crap about hurting your sister? Did Cass lie?"

"Emma broke my I-pod and I threw it—bruised her cheek a little. Made me mad because she didn't ask to use it."

Sarah moved to her next question. "Who are Emma's friends?"

"Shannon is her best friend at home. She hangs out with Lindsey and Natalia here."

"Call Lindsey and Natalia. See if they can meet us by the dive shack," Sarah instructed.

"I'll call Lindsey. Natalia doesn't have a cell, and her dad gets mad if she uses his business phone. What do I tell Lindsey?"

"Tell her we're worried because Emma still hasn't come home."

Tanner retrieved the cell phone from his pocket and punched in a number.

Lexie thought it interesting that he knew Lindsey's number without looking it up.

"Lindsey, it's Tanner. Emma's still a no show. My aunt, the detective, wants to ask you some questions."

Silence while Tanner listened.

"She doesn't bite. Wants info on Emma's hangouts and friends. Can you meet us at the dive shack in an hour? Okay, I'll tell Aunt Sarah it'll have to wait until tomorrow."

Tanner laughed, "She's afraid you'll gobble her up, Auntie."

"I only devour bad people—not your girlfriend."

"I never said she was."

"Surely, you don't memorize the numbers of all your sister's friends. How old is she?"

Tanner's rosy cheeks lightened a bit. "She's sixteen, like me."

"That's good. I don't want an older woman enticing my boy."

Tanner nudged Sarah's shoulder, "I should be so lucky."

Sarah pinched his cheek, "Smart mouth."

CHAPTER FOUR

Tye's Case

As he traveled the few miles to the high school Tye felt as if he drove through stiff air. Even though the treetops swayed, the humidity was suffocating.

As soon as Tye arrived he spotted Jim's tall, slim frame leaning on a bat. Short brunette curls escaped from the front of his backward baseball cap. Tye walked toward the baseball diamond where his father-in-law continued to put the boys through their paces even though an occasional strike of lightning streaked across the sky.

"Damn, Jim, send these guys home before the storm hits."

Jim shot a stream of tobacco out the edge of his mouth. "They'll live. Need their butts worked for that sorry ballgame last night."

"If that lightning gets any closer, they may die."

"Whatever," Jim retorted. "What are you doing here?"

"Surely, you heard about the missing girl."

"I figured Weird Wendy would've showed up by now."

"She in your class?"

"Nah, never would've known she existed if I didn't catch a glimpse of her giant knockers in her gym T-shirt that rainy day."

Tye felt the urge to cram his fist into Jim's face. "You're too old for name calling. Sexual innuendos about a minor can get you fired."

One side of Jim's lip curled but he didn't comment, so Tye continued. "May I borrow your team to search the school?"

"They're yours and thanks for the excuse to cut practice short. Make sure they get the equipment stored."

Jim turned to leave.

"Anything you want me to tell your team?"

"How about watching the slugs made me so sick I left?"

Tye waved and hollered, "Bring it in guys. I need help inside." He felt tempted to tell them their tough coach was afraid of thunder, but didn't.

Ten teen boys picked up equipment as they moved toward him. Tye knew all of them by sight and maybe half by name. The team that started with twenty players in January melted to half. Their desertion was due to Jim's hot temper and burning verbal orders.

"Guys, put the equipment away, then meet me in the front lobby."

Ten minutes later a semicircle formed around Tye and twenty eyes stared.

"Here's the deal. Wendy Elliot didn't come home after school. The school needs searched. Open every door, look in closets, and explore any place a human body might fit."

"You think she's dead?" A longhaired boy questioned.

"No," Tye answered, "I think someone played a mean trick and locked her in somewhere."

Blurred words sounded from the back of the group, then laughter.

"What's so funny?"

"Nothing," a towheaded boy responded through smiling lips.

Tye pointed to the guy beside Towhead. "You said something. What?"

"Just said that Wendy the Witch can wiggle her nose to escape."

"We don't have time for jokes," Tye snapped. "Divide into groups of three and each trio take a floor. Funny boy, you stay here."

The others gone, Tye let his stare grind into the kid's face for a few seconds. "Why did you call Wendy a witch?"

"Because she's a weird-o."

"What's strange about her?"

"She told me my dead father wanted me to stay with baseball. That's the kind of shit she spreads."

"Anything else?"

"She said Dad left me a letter in my old duffle bag."

"And?"

"It was there. She went through my personal belongings. I don't want that creep touching my stuff."

"Then what?"

"I scared her off. I told her to mind her own business or else."

"Or else what? Lance is your name, right?"

He nodded, "I wanted her trap shut."

"Has she told anyone else things they didn't want to hear?"

"I don't know."

"Go help the guys on the third floor."

Lance trotted to the stairwell.

Tye knocked on the principal's office door. "Hey Mr. Bradford any news on Wendy?"

Bradford wobbled over to shake his hand. "I haven't heard a word. Her mom has called a half dozen times. What are the baseball players doing in the school?"

"They're checking every nook and cranny. If Wendy isn't found soon: cancel school tomorrow. I'll call in law enforcement for a thorough search. These guys don't seem motivated to find her."

"Wendy's like a fly on the wall," Bradford offered. "Most people don't even realize when she's present. She's a loner, who stares into space. I received a report once that she talked to a pole."

A rotund figure with white hair and a beard appeared in the doorway. Santa Claus came to Tye's mind.

Principal Bradford motioned toward the Santa look alike. "Tye this is Trey Moore. He drives the bus Wendy rides."

Tye returned the man's firm handshake. "Was Wendy on your bus today?"

"No, sir."

"With all the kids you transport, why are you certain?"

"She's the last one off the bus. It's easy to remember since I get home sooner when she's absent."

"Have you heard any of the kids harassing her?"

Anger seeped into the driver's words. "They only pulled that shit within my earshot once. I promised them hell to pay if they didn't shut up."

Tye noted the tremor in the man's voice. "Who bothered her?"

"It was one of them cheerleaders. I think her name is Star."

"Starla," Principal Bradford corrected.

"Yep, she's the one," Moore confirmed.

The racket of running feet and loud voices ended the adult conversation.

"We didn't find Wendy," Longhair announced. "We looked everywhere. The lockers are all locked, but I don't think she'd fit in one anyway."

Tye raised his hand and voice. "Thanks guys. Hurry home—right now. A storm is coming, and I don't want your folks worried."

"Thanks for saving us from Jungle Jim," Towhead joked.

Tye didn't manage to suppress his smile. He gave a farewell wave to Bradford and Moore, then followed the team out the door. He hoped to catch an earful of gossip. Perhaps he'd hear someone's take on what happened to Wendy. However, the chatter was only about the threatening weather and getting home before it hit.

Settled into the cruiser, he checked the recent numbers—only one—and pushed it in.

Mrs. Elliot answered the phone with a breathy, "Yes."

"It's Tye, Betty."

"Have you found my girl?"

"No."

Her words turned to trembling mush.

Tye heard her husband, Clark, in the background. He apparently snatched the phone from his wife.

"Sorry. Betty's having a hard time. Any news?"

"The baseball team searched the school. The bus driver said Wendy didn't get on the bus after class. He remembered for sure, because he didn't have to drive so far out of town with the storm coming."

"We're his last stop. Moore teases us about living out in the boonies."

Tye continued, "One teacher reported that Wendy missed her history class, second session after lunch. We'll start an all out search in the morning. It's too stormy to ask folks to come out tonight."

Clark spoke in slow motion. "What do you want us to do?"

"Call your family and friends. Tell everyone we're forming a search party. Be at the sheriff's office at 7 o'clock in the morning. I think we'll get a good size group of volunteers. You and Betty hang in there."

"We will," Clark muttered.

"See you in the morning."

Sweat ran down Tye's sides. A bad feeling nudged at his brain. Why doesn't Wendy go home so her parents won't worry? Why do the guys call her a witch?

A thought motivated Tye to sprint from the patrol car and round the old brick building. It was the same high school he attended twenty-two years ago. No outside structures were near the school. A green campus merged into a wooded area backing the high school. He wandered the area. It was a necessity to search before the rain drowned evidence. He didn't find any scuff marks or disturbed greenery along the entrance to the wooded area. Tomorrow he'll have the search team start at the tree line and branch out covering every foot of the terrain. Aware of the eerie stillness in the air, and the muted yellows and pinks in the sky, he ran to the patrol car.

CHAPTER FIVE

Lexie's Case

Tanner pointed, "There's the dive shack on the right."

Sarah parked a few yards away from the building that time and weather turned gray. About twenty feet long by twelve feet wide, the shack held an array of water sports equipment. Scuba and snorkel gear dangled on hooks down the sides and across the back of the shack.

Tanner sang out, "He's the too tan guy with the weird hat."

Footsteps of the three clipped across the dirt lot. They waited patiently as Zane finished with a customer.

"What's up, Tanner? I'm working."

Lexie noted the irritation in Zane's words.

"My aunt and this lady sheriff want to ask you questions about Emma."

A cloud crossed his face, "What about Emma?"

Sarah broke in, "She's been missing since night before last. I heard you saw her right before she disappeared."

Zane turned to an older man counting money in the corner. "Break?"

"Be back in twenty minutes."

Zane came out the side door, then walked a few yards from the shack before he stopped and turned toward the threesome.

"Tanner, go get Lexie and me a couple of waters and something for yourself. I require fifteen minutes alone with Zane.

"Okay," he dragged his feet toward his assignment.

Sarah's hands rested on her waist. "Here's the deal, Zane. Emma's vanished and you're my prime suspect. Convince me that I shouldn't drag you to jail."

"I didn't hurt Emma."

Lexie rattled off a series of questions: "What happened when you two went to the beach? Why didn't you bring her home? Why did you lie about dropping her off at the movie?"

"Emma dumped me. She held my hand and kissed me twice that afternoon. Right before it was time to go home, she told me she wanted to date new guys at college. Told me to find a new girl. My guy friends told me she'd dump me sooner or later."

Lexie spoke softly, "How did you respond to that blow?"

"I didn't say anything. I left quickly, because I was about to cry. I got to my truck before the dam broke. I didn't want her to see me sobbing like a baby."

Sarah's words jabbed, "Did you even consider her safety?"

"She swims like a fish and had her cell phone. Emma already made it clear she didn't want me around."

Sarah hollered at Tanner, "Get a move on kid."

His hurried steps delivered the drinks. Sarah took one long gulp before issuing the next order. "Zane, take us to the spot where you last saw my niece."

Zane's long strides led Lexie and company towards what was Emma's last known sighting.

Lexie's eyes scanned the rocky inlet that served as access to the rolling waves. A long wooden pier jutting out from the bank allowed boats to anchor and board from its sides. "Where did you last see her, Zane?"

"When I reached the truck door, Emma was beside that boulder. Her beach bag slung over her shoulder—like she was leaving."

Lexie broke in, "Why did you tell people she was dropped off at the theater?"

"When I heard she didn't get home, I freaked because I left her alone."

A loud holler sounded from outside the dive shack.

"That's my boss. I've got to get back to work."

"We'll have more questions later." Sarah handed him her number. "If you think of anything, call me sixty seconds later."

"Yes, Ma'am." Zane jogged toward the shack.

"Let's move around a bit and search with our eyes. Don't touch anything, Tanner. If something seems out of place holler at Lexie or me."

The trio focused on the ground as they moved forward in a parallel line a yard apart.

Tanner separated from the line and moved toward the rocky entrance. A shallow screech sounded through the air, "Aunt Sarah!"

Sarah trotted toward him, "What is it?"

"There on the rocks— a backpack—like Emma's."

"Check it out, Lexie."

Lexie followed Tanner down the steep incline to the water's edge. The pack was wedged securely between two rocks. "Sure it's your sister's?"

He choked out, "Yes. See the initials on the side?"

Lexie pulled on gloves then tugged at the bag. It didn't budge. The rocks on either side gripped like a vice. It was as if someone wanted to be certain the ocean didn't float the evidence of Emma's presence away. Lexie grasped each side of the backpack and tugged with all her might. She ended up on the rocks holding the retrieved bag above her head.

"Keep looking, Tanner," Lexie urged. "There may be something else."

A few minutes later Sarah yelped from the end of the pier.

Lexie and Tanner's feet rattled the boards as they ran toward her.

"What is it, Aunt?"

"A senior ring forced into a knothole. Is it Emma's?"

Tanner's eyes filled with tears, "Yes."

"Run get the camera from the SUV and I'll take some photos," Sarah directed.

····●●●●●····

Thirty minutes later they dropped Tanner off at his front door.

"Do I have to tell Dad about the ring and backpack?"

"Yes," Sarah answered. "Lexie and I'll visit the police chief."

With head down and shoulders rounded the teen lumbered toward his front door.

Lexie moved to the front seat. "Emma wasn't really gone until he saw her belongings by the ocean."

Sarah nodded, "It wasn't real for either of us until that moment."

CHAPTER SIX

Tye's Case

The weather left Tye no recourse, but to hurry home and find a safe place to hunker down. The dust on the road spun in mini twisters. The storm's darkness engulfed the sun's last flickers of the day. He pushed the message button on his phone.

Jamie's voice squealed. "You come home right now Tye Wolfe! Diffee is in the tornado's path."

He heard his five-year-old in the background mimicking Jamie's words. "Come home right now, Daddy."

Tye watched his speedometer rise to eighty. Only the rough surface of the road kept him on track. He saw it in his rear window. The tornado chased him, ready to devour the cruiser and send him spinning into the air. A dry laugh huffed out—a spin indeed. The funnel loomed over the football field about a half-mile to his east. The sound of a nonexistent train filled the air, and then an avalanche of wood pieces attacked his vehicle. A branch hit the back window sending a spray of glass over his head. The branch point pierced through the passenger seat. Tye shook the glass from his hair and gripped the steering wheel. Old Mill Road came into view. He steered to the right and took the long way home. No doubt the stadium was flattened, but he'll check that out tomorrow.

I survived the night, provided another tornado isn't sneaking up behind or hovering in the distance to take a second shot at Diffee.

He drove through the middle of town. Everything appeared intact. Lots of lightweight stuff blown from designated places, but no major hazards were evident.

His phone blasted into the quiet.

"You okay, Tye? Where are you?"

"On my way home—quite a trip. Back window of the cruiser is broken, but I'm okay. Anymore storm warnings out?"

"You scared me to death, and poor little Gabriel is shaking." Anger and fear merged in Jamie's tone.

"Sorry, honey. I'm on my way."

Tye punched in the office number. "J.J., lock up and cruise around town. Check those two farmhouses out east and make sure the folks are okay. I'm heading home."

"I'm on it."

Tye saw his two-story farmhouse in the distance, thankful it was west of town. He and Jamie bought the place in January to make room for their adopted boys, Seth and Gabriel.

Tye painted the house beige in April, then added dark brown trim. Jamie eyed the house for forty minutes before deciding on brown paint that matched the rock sidewalk leading to the front door.

Brody and Adam came out as Tye reached the front porch.

"You guys headed out?"

"Yep," Brody responded. "According to the weatherman the storms moved past Diffee. Nothing else is forecast to hit tonight."

"The newspaper editor assigned me the tornado story, so I got to get at it," Adam explained.

Tye watched as his identical twin sons moved toward Adam's old red truck. Sons he didn't know he had until a couple of years ago. Jamie's father sent her away to have the babies. Jim didn't think a wild teenager like Tye was a suitable father, much less a partner for his teenage daughter. The babies were adopted into different families. Adam ended up in a good home. The man who called himself Brody's father molested him repeatedly over the years.

Small boys assaulted Tye with hugs as he opened the door. A pissed-off wife stood back and watched with tears in her eyes.

"I checked the woods in back of the school before the rain destroyed evidence."

Jamie fisted her apron, "Still no Wendy?"

"We'll talk after the boys are in bed."

"I warmed up your supper."

Tye wrapped his arms around her. "I love you even when you're mad."

She planted a quick peck on his cheek. "I may get over it, but don't hold your breath."

Seth tugged at his sleeve. "Did you see the tornado, Daddy?"

Tye pulled out a dining room chair. "I rode it like a cowboy on a bucking bull—up and down. That tornado tried to throw me, but I kept moving."

Gabriel giggled, "You're silly, Daddy. You can't ride a tornado."

"Oh well, I better tell the truth. I ran like a jackrabbit chased by a fox. Thank goodness the storm curved away from me."

"Good grief, husband." Jamie fit her hands around his neck. "You better stop this superman stuff or I'll choke you."

"Yes, wife. May I eat now?"

"I suppose."

Seth and Gabriel stood on either side as Tye ate. The two half brothers were as different as the twins were alike. The boys had the same mother, but Seth's skin tone indicated an Indian father and Gabriel's a white dad.

"You boys put your pajamas on," Jamie directed.

"I'll read you a book as soon as I'm finished here," Tye promised.

The pair scampered off, and Jamie sat down opposite him.

He paused his next bite, "Lance made a joke about Wendy being a witch. Do you know anything about that?"

"Never heard her called a witch. I do know she's not part of any group. Only one she ever eats with is Jason Durring.

They're a pair of outcasts. I was glad when they started hanging out together."

"Anyone particularly abrasive toward Wendy?"

"I can't think of anyone. They're not likely to harass her in earshot of a teacher. Everyone, except Jason, stays away from her."

The chair scraped against the wood floor as Tye stood. "I'll read to the boys then head to bed. Wendy's search party is gathering at 7 a.m. I'll check out the stadium damage before that. I'll leave around 5:30 in the morning."

Jamie wrapped her arms around him. He returned the hug and added a long kiss.

CHAPTER SEVEN

Lexie's Case

The SUV sped around the curves and down the straight pavement that led to the police department.

Sarah didn't take her eyes off the road. "What are your thoughts, Lexie?"

"I talked to a couple of men while I waited for you. One thought Emma's disappearance was the result of her father being one of the wealthy people who took over the community during the warm months. The second mentioned trafficking. Both are possibilities we'll pursue. Zane's the number one suspect at the moment. Too soon to rule out involvement by your family: Devon, Cass and Tanner."

Sarah's words heaved out, "They're not involved. Don't waste our time."

Lexie stared straight ahead. Sarah was no different than the general population—didn't think her relatives capable of doing harm to one of their own. Lexie determined to pursue the possibility with or without Sarah's approval.

"You don't think Cass is a concern?"

"She's a pain in the ass, but she'd never do anything to get her hands dirty."

Lexie changed the subject. "Do you think Emma's senior ring crammed in the wood knot is significant?"

Sarah's tone mellowed, "I think Em sent me a message. It took effort to push that ring in that small opening. I think she wanted me to know that she was alive."

A stretch, Lexie thought. "Any reason why you have that theory?"

Em and I talked about detective work a few times. She's a smart girl. She'd leave me a clue."

Lexie continued to think aloud. "I have no doubt that the backpack was left on purpose to give the impression that she drowned."

"I agree." Sarah stopped in front of the police station.

Lexie grabbed the evidence bag from the backseat then followed Sarah in the door.

The Police Chief wasn't expecting visitors as evidenced by the half empty vodka bottle in his hand. Droplets fell on papers as he quickly uncorked it from his sucking lips.

A nervous twitter penetrated his words, "Taking a little break." He stuck the bottle in a desk drawer. "What can I do for you ladies?"

The guy swiped a moist hand across his shirt before offering it to Sarah then Lexie. "I'm Ted Swinson."

"I'm Detective Chandler, Emma's aunt. My friend is Lexie Wolfe, a sheriff from Oklahoma. We're here to discuss Emma's disappearance."

"Don't get riled up. She's eighteen—an adult. She's probably held up with Zane somewhere getting some afternoon delight." Ted winked at Lexie.

Sarah's fist clenched at her side.

Lexie spoke, "They broke up. Zane was the last one who saw her. He's our number one person of interest."

"Zane's a good kid, and the best quarterback this town ever had."

Sarah's words singed, "Throwing a football doesn't rule him out."

Swinson's hand motioned, "What's in that bag?"

"Evidence," Sarah retorted. "Are you sober enough to get it to a lab?"

Lexie broke into the verbal sparring. "Emma's backpack was found on the shore. Someone wants us to think she drowned, or someone pushed her in."

Sarah continued, "We found her class ring stuck in a knothole where the boats load off the pier. I think she left me a clue."

"I hope you were smart enough to leave it alone."

I'm a real detective, Swinson. I know how to handle evidence."

"Well, you moved the backpack."

"I couldn't risk someone snatching it."

Swinson's pickled brain didn't think of a snotty reply. He looked longingly at his liquor drawer.

Lexie continued, "We took photos, but need the area checked for prints."

"Exactly where are we talking about?"

Sarah offered a brief description of the site.

Swinson fingered the drawer handle. "Yep, know right where that is. I'll get a man right out. We'll take care of this."

He reached for the plastic bag that housed the evidence. "I'll send this off for prints and DNA. You girls have a nice evening."

Sarah turned toward Swinson when she reached the door. "It's impossible to have a nice evening when my niece is trapped somewhere, or dead."

Swinson's hand rested on the liquor drawer knob. He didn't respond to Sarah's verbal jab.

"Son-of-a-bitch," Sarah raved as soon as the SUV engine revved. "Swinson's a do-nothing alcoholic cop."

"The good news," Lexie commented, "is it'll be easy to investigate behind his back."

"He damn sure better not hamper us or I'll find a way to screw him out of his job."

Lexie rubbed her temples. *I didn't realize Sarah was a hothead. This case is too close to home for her to be objective.*

"Let's stop and get some supper," Sarah suggested.

"Food to go—if that's okay with you. "I'd like to eat, shower and get to bed. It's been a long day."

"Works for me," Sarah agreed. "There's a burger joint on the corner."

After a quick trip to the drive through window, the smell of fries filled the vehicle.

"I'm famished, yogurt for breakfast and no lunch. Do you mind if I eat in the car? The smell is tantalizing."

"I'm thinking the same thing." Sarah drove with one hand and consumed a burger with the other. After five or six giant bites, each followed by vigorous chewing, Sarah returned to the case. "I'll call the feds in the morning. Find answers regarding sex trafficking in this area."

Lexie got the word "good" out between bites.

They pulled in front of the condo as Lexie chewed her last bite. The porch and yard lights illuminated their path. The front door was ajar. They walked into the living room.

Lexie hoped to find Emma sitting on the sofa, pleading forgiveness for causing so much worry. No Emma.

Devon's inquiring eyes met Sarah's face. "Anything?"

"I'll tell you what we've learned so far. Get some rest, Lexie. We'll leave at eight in the morning."

Devon pointed toward the stairs. "Lexie you're in Emma's room, last door on the left. Aunt Sarah, you're in the guest room on this level."

Lexie said, "Night" then dragged herself up the steps, not sure if it was possible to sleep in a room absent its girl.

CHAPTER EIGHT

Tye's Case

Tye quietly pulled the front door shut. The sun's rays hadn't yet made their presence known, which left the air a bit chilly. It was a beautiful morning, a stark contrast to the night before. The weather won't hamper the search for Wendy, and perhaps more people will join the search.

Uncertainty occupied his thoughts. He grabbed his phone in the hope of a message saying that Wendy suddenly appeared during the night. No such luck.

Tye's white Avalanche turned polka dot from sprays of mud hitting its surface as he followed the path of the tornado's destruction. Reaching the outskirts of what used to be the football stadium, his eyes searched for a parking spot free of debris. He walked toward a vacant space, where bleachers used to stand. The boards were either mulched to kindling or sucked up and carried away. The former concession stand was now a pile of rubble. A popcorn popper and an ice chest poked up from the trash. In the middle of the collapsed wood shelving, an arm stuck straight toward the sky.

"No!" shot from Tye's mouth. His heart pounded. "Wendy! I'll get you out!"

Tye flung wood pieces and twisted metal fixtures, then lifted and pushed the shelving to the side.

The girl's eyes didn't open. The hand previously held up by the spoils of the storm fell stiffly downward.

Tye knelt and felt her wrist—no pulse. He stopped and pulled gloves from his pocket, then stretched the front of Wendy's blood stained blouse apart revealing a hole in her chest.

The tornado didn't kill Wendy—someone murdered her.

Tye phoned the Oklahoma State Bureau of Investigation, then J.J. "Come to the football stadium and guard the area until help comes."

"Folks are arriving for the search, Tye."

"Wendy's dead, but don't tell anyone. Her parents need informed before the entire town knows."

"I'll be there in ten minutes."

Tye walked around the area, but there wasn't anything to see. The rain and wind swept and scrubbed the area clean of clues. *Maybe the autopsy will shed light on the killer*. He couldn't bear to look at Wendy's features frozen in death. *A life gone too soon because of some deranged fool.*

Tye heard the rattle of J.J.'s cruiser before he saw it.

His long strides moved forward. His shaved head glistened from the sun's rays. A man who showed little emotion and spoke few words, J.J.'s stoic stance faltered as his eyes focused on Wendy's face.

Tye's finger pointed to concession rubble. "Stand guard over there. OSBI will be here soon. I've got to catch Betty and Clark before they end up at the sheriff's office."

"We'll get the bastard who did this."

"We will," Tye confirmed.

He jogged toward the truck, quickly slid into the seat then drove off. The Elliot's needed told ASAP. After three miles he slowed his vehicle. *What are the words to tell a mother and father that their only child lay dead in a pile of rubble?*

He came to the only possible conclusion. There were no words to soften the blow. *Regardless of how long I think or how much I want to give them a few more minutes of peace—Wendy is gone forever.*

Tye saw the couple climbing into their truck as he parked beside their house.

He didn't walk toward them, but toward a circle of metal chairs under an oak tree.

Clark slammed the truck door then bellowed, "Tye?"

Betty followed her husband. Tye waited for Betty to catch up, then motioned for her to sit.

She shook her head. "Is Wendy hurt, Deputy?"

A chill went down Tye's spine. "I found Wendy this morning in the tornado rubble at the stadium. She's dead."

Betty's shriek pierced the air. She fell to her knees. "My baby—my baby—my baby is dead."

Clark didn't try to comfort her. His skin was as colorless as his white T-shirt. "If we searched last night we'd have found her before the tornado hit. I knew I should've gone, but I held up in a cellar, while my girl died."

Tye's voice was firm, "There wasn't anything you could do."

Clark protested, "I might have found her in time."

"The storm didn't kill Wendy. She was murdered before the storm hit."

"Murdered!" the word roared from Clark.

An ear-piercing scream escaped Betty's mouth.

The father's fist throbbed in the air. "Who? Why would anyone hurt my girl? She's a harmless child."

"I don't know why, but I'll find the monster."

"I'll find him first," Clark threatened. "There'll be nothing left of him, but a pile of body parts."

"It's my job. You take care of Betty."

Clark's eyes blazed hate, but he made no more threats. He pulled Betty to standing. The men supported her on either side into the house.

"Wendy's room," she whimpered.

The mother sat on the edge of the bed then rolled flat against the pink spread. Her face sank into the pink heart pillow with a cross embroidered in the middle. Whimpers turned to sobs, then screams of disbelief.

Clark waved Tye out the bedroom door, then shut it behind them. He sat stiffly on a wood rocker.

Tye opened the outside door, "I'll keep you informed."

Clark didn't respond. As the door closed behind him, Tye heard the wretched moan of a heartbroken man.

It was a thirty-minute drive back to his office. Tye parked in the handicapped space by the front door, the only spot left.

Vehicles lined both sides of Main Street. Dixie's restaurant lot was also packed.

He ignored the "hellos" as he made his way past the men congregating outside the office.

Delia flurried about inside. She handed out paper cups filled with coffee or water. Her eyes met Tye's and she knew the truth.

"Where are Clark and Betty?" A man's voice rang out and others mimicked his question with "Yes."

Tye raised a quieting hand. He waited a minute as the men from outside came into the crowded office.

"First, I'd like to thank you all for coming. It makes me proud that so many people are willing to help their neighbors."

"Cut to the chase, Tye. What's up?" A voice barked from the back of the crowd.

Tye's somber voice delivered the message. "Wendy Elliot was found dead this morning."

"Oh, no" and "bless her folks" filled the air.

A teenage voice piped in loudly, "Caught in the tornado?"

"No. Wendy was murdered."

The sprinkling of kind comments from before became an eruption of disbelief and horror. Individual words clumped into an incomprehensible mass in Tye's head.

A father's voice rose above the crowd racket. "What's going on Tye? Are our daughters in danger?"

"I don't know. The Oklahoma Bureau of Investigation is already at the site for the initial investigation. Keep your children home until we know more."

"Did you tell Clark and Betty?" Delia asked.

Tye nodded the affirmative.

"I can't even imagine the pain they're facing." Delia emptied computer paper from a box then put the two parts on a desk. "If you have a cash donation put it in the box. Betty's sister, Sue, can take it to them.

Members of the search party trooped by the desk and donated a buck or two, or ten or twenty. Soon the room emptied except for Tye, Delia, and Sue.

Sue counted the last twenty. "Three hundred and fifty-three dollars total; that'll help pay for the funeral. I'll take it to them. Don't know if I can hold it together when I get there."

Delia patted her back, "You'll do fine."

"I hope," Sue answered.

After walking Sue to the door, Delia waited as Tye texted a message.

"You telling Lexie?"

"Yes, she'll want an update."

"Figured," Delia sat down at her desk.

"I'll replace J.J. at the site and assist the investigative team. Call me if anything comes up."

Tye didn't see Delia's nod as he rushed into the sunny day. The weather didn't reflect his disposition or the town's sorrow.

He forced himself to slow down. He didn't understand why he was frantic to get there—too late for Wendy.

CHAPTER NINE

Lexie's Case

Lexie slept soundly. Something she didn't expect in a strange bed in a room absent its teenage girl. She lifted a photo from the nightstand. Emma didn't inherit the Chandler husky built. She was petite with long blonde hair that touched her shoulders. Her arms enclosed a slender woman, the same height, with a kerchief wrapped head—likely the last photo taken of the two prior to her mom's death from breast cancer.

Emma looked like a fifteen-year-old, not eighteen. Sarah said she was 5 feet 1 inch and maybe a hundred pounds.

Lexie's cell phone clicked. Two messages from last night showed up on the screen. She pushed the voicemail button. "Everything is okay here. The tornado hit east of town. It took out the stadium and the empty motel." The rhythm in Lexie's chest escalated. Red's voice continued, "Sky is fine. She slept through the storm. She's a deep sleeper like me." Her heartbeat slowed.

Delia delivered the next message, "We're good, but your stubborn brother got so close to the tornado he had to race away."

Somehow Lexie missed the Diffee tornado news. For the best, probably, since she would've worried about Sky all night. Even though she knew Red kept her safe. It was scary to learn that her town could've disappeared while she slept.

She sent Red and Delia texts, then a one-word message to Tye: Wendy?

Lexie sat on the zebra print comforter and visually studied Emma's room. It was decorated in all things black-and-white with splashes of red. Red sheers hung between zebra drapes. Red pompoms set on either side of her cheerleading photo situated in the middle of the dresser.

Perhaps, eventually, she'll examine the contents of the drawers and closet for clues. But, at the moment, it seemed invasive to handle the girl's private belongings. She'll wait.

Lexie pulled on blue jeans and a sleeveless red T-shirt. She brushed and braided her hair, then stuck her feet into blue tennis shoes before heading downstairs.

The living room was empty. She caught sight of Sarah and Devon on the patio. The pair looked up when she slid the door open.

"Did you sleep well, Lexie?" Devon asked.

"I did."

Sarah motioned toward a white metal table. "There's pastries and fruit for breakfast."

Lexie dished a serving of fruit onto a small glass plate. She joined her host and Sarah in a circle of green and blue upholstered patio chairs.

"Any news overnight?" She shouldn't have asked since the answer was apparent from the dark bags that drooped under Devon's eyes.

"Nothing," Sarah answered. "I phoned the feds. They connected me to a sex trafficking agent." A mischievous smile played at Sarah's lips. "I mentioned your name, Lexie, and he was motivated to get here as soon as possible."

"I don't know anyone who works trafficking cases."

"You do now; Stan Johnson will arrive late this afternoon."

"You've got to be kidding." *Why did I ever tell Sarah about my almost affair with Stan?*

Devon's voice peaked in concern. "Is this guy a do-nothing?"

"He knows his stuff," Lexie assured Devon. "I worked with him a couple of times when he was a detective in D.C. Apparently, he's made a career change."

Devon pursued, "What's wrong with the guy?"

Sarah broke in, "He's a sexist jerk and lady law enforcement would like to get his penis clipped."

Devon chuckled, "I feel sorry for the man. I may have to give him some brotherly support."

"If you do, nephew, you're going to get your ass kicked."

Devon's momentary cheer faded. "But you say he's a good cop?"

"He's all business when it comes to work." Lexie looked at Sarah. "What's our plan today?"

"We'll take off in a few minutes and visit Emma's girlfriends. Johnson's flight gets at 4:15 this afternoon."

Tanner's slumped body entered through the sliding door. He wore swim trunks and a T-shirt. A blue duffle bag was slung over his shoulder.

Devon's words hacked out, "Where the hell do you think you're going?"

Tanner's eyes bore into his father's angry face. "I'm going to the beach and ask questions about my sister. Where are you going—work, as usual?"

"Sorry, son."

"Better if you don't go off alone, Tanner. For all we know Emma's disappearance may be a vendetta against your family."

"You really think that's possible, Aunt Sarah?"

"Probably not, Devon, but it's too soon to rule out."

Tanner sulked, "I can't stay here all day and do nothing."

"Come with us. Show us where we can find those two friends of Emma's."

"Okay."

"Let's head out, team."

Lexie grabbed a banana and followed Sarah and Tanner through the house. *Wonder where the lady of the estate is?*

"Do you expect these girls on the beach today? Sarah aimed the question at Tanner.

"Lindsey said she'd be there. Natalia's dad won't let her out alone since her sisters died."

"Amos? I met him on the beach yesterday."

"That's him," Tanner verified. "I feel sorry for Natalia. Her father has her trapped."

"It's only been a few months," Lexie offered. "Surely he'll let up soon."

"She hopes so," Tanner said.

The road to Natalia's house made their vehicle grumble and the tires squeal. The road curled down to an inlet. A rope anchored a houseboat turned fishing boat to a rotting post.

The weather-ravaged house stood several yards from the water's edge. Amos looked up from his bait bucket as they walked toward him."

The man's voice heaved, "I told you, Tanner, Natalia can't go out."

"I know, sir. This is my Aunt Sarah and her friend, Lexie. They're trying to find my sister."

Amos nodded toward Lexie then faced Tanner. "I heard about your sister's disappearance, boy. Your dad should've kept her close to home."

"They have questions for Natalia."

"Natalia's safe at the house, not out with Emma since last summer."

"We have questions about where Emma likes to go, and if there's anyone she dislikes. Teenagers tell their friends more than adults," Lexie explained.

"Figures," Amos grunted. "Go to the door and holler for her, Tanner. Her mom and grandma went to the grocery store."

Tanner ran to the door, pulled open the screen and yelled, "Natalia."

"Come on out," Tanner directed when she appeared in the doorway.

"But Dad?"

"He told me to get you."

The teens made their way toward the adults. Unlike all the tan teenagers Lexie had seen on her trip, Natalia's skin was pale—untouched by the sun. Her short blonde hair framed blue eyes and perfect features.

Tanner introduced her to the two women. "They want to know if you've heard anything about Emma."

"Dad told me she was missing, which made him more determined to keep me a prisoner."

"Hush, girl. You're not a prisoner. You're safe."

Natalia's nostrils flared.

Amos' finger shook toward her. "That's enough girl!"

"My attitude is a result of house-a-phobia."

"Is there such a thing?" Tanner asked.

"There is now," Natalia giggled.

Lexie butted into the conversation before red-faced Amos erupted. "Natalia, did Emma talk about any boys other than Zane?"

"He's her summer guy. I don't know of anyone else."

Lexie continued, "Did she ever talk about being afraid of anyone?"

"No, but I've been out of the loop since last summer. Lindsey is the one you need to ask."

"We'll do that," Sarah turned toward the SUV.

"Thanks for your time." Lexie followed Sarah's back to the vehicle.

Amos ignored Lexie's farewell, but Natalia flittered her fingers.

Lexie heard Amos yell at Natalia, "Get back in the house, girl."

Sarah spoke as she drove the SUV toward the highway. "I should kidnap Natalia. Her old man is bonkers."

Lexie turned toward Tanner. "Are her grandmother and mother on board with Amos?"

"From what I heard, her mom is a zombie since she lost two daughters. Granny cooks, cleans, and keeps her mouth shut. 'Understandable' is her only response when people ask why he won't let Natalia go out."

"I feel bad for the kid," Sarah concluded, "but we have our girl to worry about. Remind me where to turn off, Tanner."

"It's another three miles."

Less than five minutes later Sarah parked the vehicle in a space a few yards from the surf shack.

Lexie noted the two faces behind the counter, neither of which belonged to Zane.

The women followed Tanner across the gravel to a rock path that wound toward the beach.

"Hey, Lindsey," Tanner yelled.

She rolled to her back on a striped beach towel then sat up. "Any news about Emma?"

"None," Tanner answered.

"I thought she'd show up by now." Lindsey pulled a tank top over her bikini.

"This is my Aunt Sarah and Sheriff Lexie. They're looking for her."

Lindsey stood, "Are you the detective?"

"One and the same," Sarah answered.

"Emma told me about her gun toting aunt."

"Glad I got a little air time in your conversation."

"She thinks you're cool and wants to be a detective like you."

Lexie tried to imagine petite Emma scaring a criminal into obedience. She herself had enough difficulty at six inches taller and twenty-five pounds heavier.

Sarah asked, "Where do you think Emma might be?"

"I looked everywhere I could think of and called all our friends. I didn't find out anything."

Lexie asked the next question. "Did you know she planned to breakup with Zane?"

"She dreaded the drama, but was ready to move on."

"You know of any problems at home?" Lexie questioned.

Lindsey turned apprehensive eyes to Tanner. "I don't know."

"You're lying and we don't have time for it. Emma may be in danger." Sarah handed Tanner a bill, "Go get water bottles."

He grabbed the ten and ran toward the shack.

Lexie figured he knew Sarah wanted him out of earshot, but he planned to return in a flash.

"He's gone, tell us the truth," Lexie stated.

"I don't rat on my best friend."

Sarah's eyes darkened, "Emma may be dying and you're worried about gossip."

Lexie spoke calmly, "Lindsey, we'll not divulge the information. Tell us before Tanner gets back."

Words blurted out, "Emma caught her stepmother wrapped around the yard guy. She was fighting mad, but didn't know whether to tell her dad or not. He went through hell because of her mom's illness and death."

Sarah moved a step toward the girl. "Did they know she saw them?"

"Emma said she threw her purse at them and anything else she could get hold of. She said Cass screamed it was nothing. That guy, Kent, told Emma he better not lose his job over a hug."

"Then what happened?"

"That's all I know."

Tanner ran toward them. Sweat dripped from his forehead.

Sarah handed her card to Lindsey. "That's all for now. If you hear from Emma, or think of anything else, call me."

Tanner handed out the bottles, then tromped behind the women. When the threesome settled back in the vehicle, he snarled, "Did she give you any information?"

Sarah responded, "All we have are questions—no answers."

"Right," Tanner said with doubt.

Lexie spoke up, "Is there anyone who works for your parents on a regular basis?"

"Cleaning lady is Bertha. She's almost eighty. Kent does yard work, maintenance, and takes care of the condo when we're gone."

Sarah joined in, "Anyone else? Is someone angry at your dad or Cass?"

"You think someone took Emma to make Dad suffer?"

"It's possible," Sarah noted.

"I don't know who my stepmom hangs out with. It's her first summer here. I don't think she has friends. Everyone likes Dad."

"Do Kent and Bertha get along with all of you?" Lexie asked.

"Dad told Emma to stay away from Kent."

Sarah's eyes flashed, "Why?"

"Because she doesn't like him. Emma told Dad he should get rid of him. Dad said he wouldn't fire a good worker."

Sarah's hands tightened on the wheel as she pulled in front of the condo. "I'll drop you off then Tanner and I'll get Johnson at the airport. It should take about an hour total."

Lexie didn't have to hear the words. She knew Sarah wanted her to follow-up on the Cass/Kent thing. She stopped and viewed a text.

The message from Tye was short and painful. Wendy Elliot is dead: murdered.

CHAPTER TEN

Tye's Case

Tye arrived at the murder site after what looked like half the town's men.

Houser, from the Oklahoma State Bureau of Investigation, reprimanded the men loudly for parking near, and tromping through, the murder site. J.J. stood a few yards in front of Houser. J.J's arms spread like wings signaling the crowd to stand back.

Tye elbowed through the men and climbed to the top of a debris pile. "Do you men want responsibility for destroying evidence?" Get out of here before I hand out tickets."

"Damn," a bearded guy yapped. "You wouldn't do that."

Tye retrieved a form from his pocket, signed it and passed it to big mouth.

"I ain't paying a hundred dollar fine."

"If someone murdered your daughter, would you want big footed men tromping evidence?"

The loud mouth shut and the rubberneckers meandered off alone or in groups of two or three.

Tye jumped from the pile.

"Where've you been, Wolfe? I'm not in the mood to deal with these Okie vigilantes," Houser puffed.

Sarcasm dripped from Tye's words. "I spent an enjoyable morning telling parents that their daughter was murdered."

"Come look at this," Houser ordered.

"You aren't my first priority."

Tye signaled J.J. "Go to your patrol car and write down the names of every man you saw here this morning. Drop the list off with Delia before you go home to sleep."

"You think the killer showed up here?"

"If a Diffee person did it, he'd want information. If a stranger murdered Wendy, he's long gone."

"Makes sense," J.J. acknowledged. "Jason Durring asked for you earlier. He said the Elliot girl was his best friend."

"Is he still around?"

"There," J.J. pointed, "leaning against that tree."

"I'll get to him, eventually."

Tye returned to Houser's bad attitude. "Found anything?"

"It'll take hours to move each piece one by one to reach the bottom."

"Is her lower body still trapped in the mess?" Tye asked.

Houser's attitude simmered, "Yes, we're going slow."

"Where did that come from?" Tye pointed to a rose thrown a few feet from the death pile.

"I guess a mourner left a commemorative flower."

"Or the killer," Tye stated.

The detective's cheeks turned rosy, "Damn."

"Anything with the flower?"

"I don't know. One of the guys flung it aside."

"Perhaps you should supervise your men instead of griping at me." Houser didn't respond to the truth.

Tye jogged to Jason, then crouched under a tree. Jason tried to do the same, but his leg muscles gave way, and his butt flattened on the earth.

Jason stood six feet three or four inches. The kid easily weighed over three hundred pounds. Jason looked like a professional linebacker, but without muscles to control his bulky body. He walked with a waddle and sat with a splat. There was probably a good looking kid beneath the facial pockets of fat and the flab that dangled beneath his chin.

"Deputy Wolfe, I want to help. Wendy was my best friend."

"As in girlfriend? Dated?"

"We weren't that kind of friends. Wendy called us kindred souls," Jason explained.

"What does that mean, Jason?"

"We're unpopular, belittled, and harassed by the other kids. We only had each other. Once we went to a football game together. One guy called us cruel names. He told us not to have freak babies together. Wendy held her cross in front of his face and said 'May God forgive you.' That shut him up."

"Anyone particularly hate Wendy? Threaten her?"

"Some of the kids called her Wendy the Witch. They accused her of sneaking around their stuff."

"Do you think she got in their things?"

"I never saw her snooping, but it was creepy how she knew things."

"For instance?"

"She told Lance his dead father gave her a message to tell him to stop doing drugs. Guy went berserk and cussed Wendy. He warned her to keep her mouth shut or else."

"Or else what?"

"Lance implied he'd hurt her."

"Did any other kids threaten her?"

"Wendy told me that Starla and Cara stuck her head in the toilet. They stopped when the bell rang."

"Why were they mad?"

"Wendy called it girl stuff and wouldn't tell me."

"Did Wendy show any anger toward the girls?"

"She squeezed her big cross and asked God to forgive them." Moisture settled under Jason's eyes. "They didn't deserve forgiveness. Both of them belong in hell."

"Did she mention adults who gave her a hard time?"

Jason picked at the grass. "I don't know if I should say."

"Of course you should tell me. I'm making you my junior deputy."

"For real, Mr. Wolfe?"

"You'll be perfect. Teenagers aren't going to speculate who killed Wendy around me. I bet you'll hear an earful of possibilities if you're on alert."

"I want to catch Wendy's killer."

"The first order of business is to tell me why you hesitated earlier."

Jason looked in the distance. "Wendy said that Coach Jim stared at her boobs."

"Did Wendy have large breasts?"

Jason's eyes brightened, "Big ones for sure, but she never let me see or touch them."

Tye ignored Jason's boob enthusiasm. "It's better if your peers don't see you hanging around me. They'll be suspicious and call you a snitch or worse."

"Better than what they already call me—Lumpster and Blubber to name a couple."

"This is about more than name calling. This is about a killer who may decide you're a threat." Tye handed Jason his personal cell phone number. "Starting Monday, check in with me every day after school. Be sure no one is listening."

"I'll do it, Deputy."

"Thanks, Jason."

Tye reached a hand as the boy struggled to get up. "Remember, just listen to what's said. Don't go sneaking around."

"Yes, Boss," he answered. His body swayed from side to side as he walked toward his old panel truck.

Tye glanced at the death pile before getting in his truck. Houser's team can take care of the tedious hunt for clues. I have a locker to search and a visit to Wendy's folks on my To Do List.

Four marked sheriff cruisers from surrounding counties lined up in front of the high school. They came, as promised, to search the building before the teachers showed up for locker checks. Opening the locks on three hundred plus lockers was a huge task. However, Tye appreciated that Diffee High School didn't have a thousand kids like some of the big city schools.

Principal Bradford met him at the door with the combination to Wendy's locker. Tye followed as Bradford led the way to the gray metal wall box on the second floor. Tye put on gloves then clicked in the numbers.

The small shelf on top was filled with a biology book, an English book, and six spirals with designated subjects written in print across the front of each. A black cross hung from the coat hanger. Typed on a sheet of yellowed paper taped on the inside of the door were three sentences:

When I fade keep me in your light.
Pull me from the shadows.
Guard my soul from darkness.

Tears welled in his eyes. Finally composed, he turned to Bradford. "Where's a box I can put this stuff in?"

"I'll have the janitor bring one up."

Janitor Gene reached them, box in hand, within four minutes of Bradford's cell phone request.

"Found anything?" he asked. "Nothin' was out of place when I cleaned early this morning."

Tye felt fire rising in his chest. "Weren't you told to stay out of the school?"

"Principal told me, but I clean up early every morning. I got to get my work done. I looked around."

Tye shook his head.

Bradford's patient words hurried out. "Go back to work, Gene. Thanks for the box."

Gene out of sight, Tye turned his anger toward Bradford. "What the hell?"

"Gene has cognitive disabilities. He doesn't think logically at times—forgets. He didn't mean any harm. He has a work pattern he follows and doesn't deviate from it."

Tye sighed, "He may have destroyed evidence."

"I thought Wendy died at the stadium."

"I cover all the bases. You never know what may lead to a killer." He packed the books and the rest of Wendy's locker contents into the cardboard box.

"Do you need anything else from me, Tye?"

"That's all for now. My next stop is Clark's place."

Bradford patted Tye's back, "I wouldn't want that visit."

"Me either," Tye answered.

CHAPTER ELEVEN

Lexie's Case

Lexie rang the condo doorbell, but no one answered. She circled the structure, then stopped abruptly at the sound of voices. She peeked around the corner and saw Cass reclining on a flowered lounger. A man looked down on her from standing. Lexie speculated the muscled guy was Kent.

"Kent, what did you do with Emma?"

He flat handed her drink off the side table. "Don't use that bitch tone with me."

"I know you threatened her."

"I wanted her mouth shut."

"Did you shut it?"

"You've got more to lose than me. A woman like you can't function without a rich husband."

Her words boiled, "What kind of woman is that?"

"The narcissistic lazy variety."

"Get out of here you S.O.B. If I find out you hurt Emma I'll have your head on a platter."

"Same to you, bitch."

Much to Lexie's relief, Kent left in the opposite direction from her hiding place. She gave him a little time then strolled around the corner.

"Lexie?" The woman's voice hit a weird crescendo. "Where are Sarah and Tanner?"

"Sarah dropped me off then left for the airport to pick up the trafficking agent."

"I'll call Bertha to get you a drink."

"No thanks. What's going on between you and the yard guy?"

"What are you talking about? Who's spreading gossip about me?"

"I heard you two arguing. Sounded like a lover's quarrel." Lexie smiled.

"He's not my lover. He's a friend."

Lexie licked her lips, "A male friend who looks that good is hard to resist."

"Devon's always a dreary, cloudy day. Kent makes me laugh."

"He wasn't cheerful five minutes ago. Do you think he knows what happened to Emma?"

She whimpered, "I don't know. He was mad—afraid he'd lose his job because Emma caught him hugging me. Of course, she thought we were having an affair."

"Emma disappeared before she had a chance to tell Devon. Don't you thing that's a strange coincidence?"

"I don't think Kent hurt her."

"How about you, Cass? Would you do away with Emma to save your marriage?"

"Don't you dare speak to me that way!" Cass swirled her legs and sat on the lounger edge. "Kent hugged me. I didn't return his affection. He's the hired help and no threat to my marriage. Get away from me. I'm under too much strain. My dear daughter is missing and you're treating me like a criminal."

This woman has righteous indignation down to an art.

"You're not welcome here, Sheriff. Pack up and get out."

"I'm not here at your invitation." Lexie moved toward the back door. "By the way, I won't divulge your secret... yet."

Her words flipped from anger to pleading, "Devon's been hurt enough. Please don't tell him. He may misinterpret the relationship like you did."

"Time will tell." Lexie let the door slam behind her.

Climbing the stairs to Emma's room she wondered if Lindsey sexualized the relationship between Cass and Kent. *Perhaps Emma jumped to the wrong conclusion, or Cass is a lying cheat.*

Back in Emma's room, Lexie flopped onto the bed and stared at the ceiling.

Now there were two more suspects, plus Zane, plus a hundred or so town's people who felt invaded by the summer crowd. The case looked more and more complicated even without the human trafficking angle. The few days she promised to help Sarah now looked like a pitiful offering.

Lexie rolled from the bed and slipped her hand under the red lampshade to flip on the light. "Tell me something, Emma," she whispered.

Emma's wasn't the expected teen room. Underwear was in one drawer, tops in another, and shorts a third—all folded neatly. A box of letters and cards in the closet didn't reveal any hate mail or perversions. Emma was a teenage girl excited about starting college and beginning her adult life. Prettier than many, and a valedictorian plaque leaned against her mirror proved she was also smarter than most. Those jealous of her accomplishments likely lived in her hometown, not at her summer home where she's one more girl on the beach.

The room offered no clues. Lexie punched Red's number into her cell phone.

A masculine voice answered.

"What are you and Sky up to?"

"Banging balls with a hammer and eating mashed carrots with a side of applesauce. You ever taste any of this junk we feed our baby?"

Lexie laughed, "Once was enough."

"More than enough as far as I'm concerned. How's your case going?"

"Suspects are here, there and everywhere. Will you hold the phone up to Sky's ear?"

"Sure thing," he answered. Lexie heard his words to Sky. "It's your mommy."

"How's my sweet baby?" A singsong tone expressed Lexie's words.

"Mama," a sweet voice said.

Lexie felt a tear sneak down her cheek. "Mama misses you and loves you."

Red came back on the line. "Sky's little face is all puckered. I think she misses you."

"Not as much as I miss her. I'll come home in a few days. Sarah will have to find a new partner."

Red's next words hurried over the line. "Gina's at the door. She's going to the park with Sky and me. See you soon."

Lexie didn't get a "bye" out before the phone line went dead. *What's he doing with Gina? He hardly knows her, and he's taking her on a picnic with my baby.*

Her chest ached. Maybe someday, maybe never, she'll accept that Red moved on. Perhaps he'll sever all emotional attachment to the sheriff who used his DNA to confirm his father was a murderer. Gina may be the final stab that kills her last hope that Red will ever come back.

A knock sounded at the door.

"Lexie?"

She straightened her clothes.

"You in there?"

Lexie opened the door, "What's up, Tanner?"

"Aunt Sarah wants you downstairs. She's taking off with that Stan guy to search the area where Emma disappeared."

Lexie grabbed her purse and followed Tanner to the waiting car.

"You stay home this time," Sarah directed through the vehicle window.

"Ah, come on," Tanner begged, "I want to go."

"No. You head back into the condo. The adults need to talk."

CHAPTER TWELVE

Tye's Case

Tye stopped at the convenience store for a chicken sandwich and coffee. Caffeine might keep his heart pumping. During his sleepless night, a jigsaw puzzle formed in his head. A dead girl was in the center of the puzzle surrounded by nothing. Soon he hoped to find the pieces to solve the murder, but at the moment it seemed unlikely. His current theory was that Wendy knew something that the murderer didn't want told, so he made sure she didn't. The first question was: How did Wendy find out the secret?

The lunch excuse finished, he drove toward Clark's place. In most parts of the country they'd be labeled as living in poverty. Their two-bedroom house wasn't much more than a shack. Flowers planted down the sides of a rock walk brightened up the worn exterior. As with most people in Diffee, poverty wasn't a word Clark or Betty applied to themselves. Homegrown food, a roof over their heads, and family was all they needed to survive.

Tye knocked on the front door.

Clark answered with raccoon eyes and a hair stubble face. "Come in and have a seat. Any news, Tye?"

"Nothing yet, but we're working on it. Sheriffs from bordering counties, teachers, and OSBI officers are all searching in and around the high school."

"Tell them I said thanks."

"Ask Betty to join us," Tye requested.

"I don't think she can handle questions. She can't stop crying and screaming."

"No choice," Tye said flatly.

Clark paused at the door to Wendy's bedroom and hollered his words. "Get out here Betty and talk to the deputy."

"Leave me be," she ranted.

"I won't," his voice scalded. "We got to help catch our girl's killer."

Betty appeared in the living room. Her swollen face was surrounded by a disheveled mass of brown hair. She wore the same striped dress from yesterday, now wrinkled and torn. She'd used the dress to vent her sorrow. She sat on the plaid sofa while Clark sank into the recliner the couple bought at Jamie's garage sale a few months earlier.

Tye sat in a stiff chair across from the couple. "This is hard stuff, Betty, but I need your help."

Betty's hands squeezed tightly together in her lap.

Tye's calm tone filled the room. "I heard a strange story regarding secrets Wendy knew. Some folks think she snooped, and found out bad things people didn't want told."

Tye looked at Betty, who looked at her husband.

Clark spoke, "I told Wendy to mind her own business. We're not supposed to interfere in other folks' lives." He focused a sharp look on his wife.

Betty shook her head, "You didn't understand our daughter."

"I knew she needed to stay out of other people's problems, so things like this wouldn't happen."

Irritation seeped into Tye's words. "What are you two talking about?"

Betty's voice gained strength, "Wendy had powers."

Tye's eyes met Clark's. "Powers?"

"I know it sounds crazy, Deputy, but it's true. It started at five years. Wendy screamed that ghosts talked to her. We took her to a psychologist to get cured."

Betty broke in, "After Wendy's second session he called us in to talk. We figured he wanted her hospitalized. Instead he told us that it wasn't mental illness. Wendy communicated with the dead. The psychologist called her a psychic medium."

Clark continued, "The psychologist said Wendy gave him a message from his dead mother. She told the doctor where his mother hid a diamond ring he'd searched for the last ten years. He found it in a Kerr jar in the attic, right where Wendy said."

"The psychologist said our daughter had a special gift and told Wendy the same," Betty added.

Tye noted the anguish in Clark's voice and the pride in Betty's.

"I wanted Wendy to help folks, but Clark said 'people won't understand' and now I know he was right."

"If you ordered her not to use her power, why did she?"

Betty stared at her hands as she spoke. "The next few years she did as her dad ordered. Last year, on television, she saw a woman who used her power to help people. Wendy decided not to waste a God given gift."

Tye tried to keep the disbelief out of his tone. "Do you have any idea what she told people?"

Betty's accusing eyes found Clark's face. "Her dad would hear none of it, so Wendy kept her secrets."

Tye stood, "I'll go through Wendy's stuff. Maybe there's something from a person angry enough to kill her."

Betty shrilled, "No! You can't touch her things."

"If you don't give me permission, I'll get a search warrant. The only thing we can do for Wendy is arrest her killer."

"Go ahead, Tye. When you're finished, lock up."

"Will do."

"Brush your hair wife. We're going into town to find a casket for our girl."

Ten minutes later Tye heard the couple exit the house. He looked out Wendy's window. The couple walked six feet apart toward the truck. Their body language conveyed more than sorrow—anger. Perhaps Clark was upset because his wife had the luxury of letting her grief out. Tye ravaging through Wendy's belongings probably brought on Betty's stiff walk.

Not much to go through in Wendy's small room. A cracked, four-drawer chest held an array of miscellaneous clothing in the top three drawers. The bottom compartment held a collection of crosses, probably a dozen. Some looked pure gold, others silver, a couple drawn on construction paper and still others roughly fashioned from wood or clay—crosses of every size and material. One oak cross was wrapped in a red scarf.

Tye knew this family couldn't afford anything gold. So where did Wendy get them—stolen? There'd never been a cross theft reported in Diffee.

He pulled on plastic gloves and examined each piece closely. Finally, his eyes spied some identifying marks. First, he discovered the initials A.M. engraved on the one-inch gold cross. Second, *Bles U* was printed in childlike letters on the back of the homemade oak cross. He assumed the writer meant 'Bless You.' These two were the only crosses that gave any hint as to where they came from.

The closet revealed nothing, nor did a fruitless search under the bed. Back in the truck, he pondered Wendy's weird case. Wendy being a witch was as illogical as her talking to dead people. Stealing crosses seemed more like a witch activity than one for God's messenger. Somewhere he'll find clues to solve the murder. Unfortunately, anything rational involving this case was in short supply.

He glanced at a text message. It revealed a second reason to stop at Lance's house before he returned to the office.

Five years ago, Lance's father died in a freak tractor accident. Lance was fourteen at the time. He dropped out of school the year his father died. Some thought it was because his mom, Lana, freaked out. Others said Lance couldn't cope with his father's death. A year later the boy showed back up at school.

Tye knocked soundly.

Lance opened the door with a wide sweep. "Mom isn't here. She's at work."

"I came to see you."

Lance stepped onto the porch. "What's this about?"

"Shouldn't be difficult to figure out since I found a dead classmate of yours at the football stadium."

"Wendy's dead?"

Tye studied his face. The kid didn't seem shocked or the least bit sad. "Do you have any thoughts on who hated Wendy enough to kill her?"

"Probably someone she spread shit about."

"Like you?"

"Hell, I didn't kill that witch."

"You're my number one suspect based on your hateful remarks at the high school."

"I wanted her out of my face."

"She's for sure out of your life now."

"You've got nothing on me."

"I received an interesting text on the way over here. The teachers did a locker check. Someone found marijuana in your locker."

Lance chewed at his bottom lip.

"I'm here to arrest you on possession charges—not murder—not yet anyway."

"I'll call Mom."

"You're nineteen, an adult. I'm not required to inform her before taking you in. You can phone her when we get to the sheriff's office."

Lance dragged his feet across the stone driveway to Tye's truck and boosted himself in.

"I thought Wendy said your dad wanted you to stay away from drugs."

"I don't believe that garbage. Do you?"

Tye eyeballed the side of his face. "I didn't...not sure anymore. How did Wendy know about your drug use?"

"Must have eavesdropped."

"I imagine it made you feel mighty guilty when she gave you the message from your father."

"My dad is dead as a rock. If he sent messages, he'd send them to Mom, not a strange girl."

"I've heard Wendy has been 'right on' before."

"You're a deputy and you believe ESP shit?"

"I'll check out the stories."

Lance's words choked out after a sudden realization. "Will this keep me from graduating next week? I could lose my baseball scholarship."

"Likely so," Tye agreed.

"What if I helped you?"

"For all I know, you're the killer."

His words earnest, "I swear I'm not. Some places have community service. Can I do that?"

"A judge decides that, Lance. Not me."

"I'm popular at school. Most kids know I've done drugs. It's common knowledge that Wendy pissed me off. They'll think I'm on their side if they hurt Wendy."

Lance had a point—smart kid. College was a good place for him unless prison was his future.

Sounds of rocks spitting from the tires and the smooth grumble of the truck's engine filled the cab.

Lance breathed out and in through an open mouth. "You knew my dad, didn't you?"

"Don't play the dead dad card, Lance. Your father was a good man and you're obviously not headed that direction."

"I got his genes. I can be a good man; if you give me a chance."

Tye twisted the wheel and made a wide U-turn. "If you have any doubt, Lance, that your dad is watching over you, this is your proof. I'm doing this for him."

The boy didn't speak, but Tye caught a moist glimmer in his eyes.

"Listen around school, then report back at the end of the day. No heroics: this person is a killer. If I find out you're working outside my parameters our deal is over. I'll haul your ass in front of a judge for possession."

"Thank you." Lance slid out of the truck as soon as Tye braked.

Tye did the same.

Lance's forehead wrinkled, "Something else?"

"Go in your house, then your car, collect all the drugs and hand them over."

"Yes, sir."

"Don't screw with me—get all of it."

Lance trotted to his car, pulled a bag from a wheel well and tossed it to Tye. After fifteen minutes in the house he returned with a brown paper bag.

Lance reached the bag toward him, "Here it is."

"That's strike one. Go get the last one—the one you planned to use before you quit."

Lance's eyes widened. He ran into the garage and returned with one small bag. "Sorry."

"Last chance," Tye warned. "Don't blow it."

"I won't."

Tye crawled back into his vehicle. A salute to Lance, then he traveled toward town. A touch of apprehension prickled his brain. *I gave my primary suspect permission to gather evidence. This may backfire, but with any luck, Lance will hang himself in a fake attempt to solve the case.*

CHAPTER THIRTEEN

Lexie's Case

Johnson stood outside the SUV. Lexie's thoughts were the same as the first time she'd seen Stan a couple of years back—best looking man ever. In the past, she was more attracted to the muscular body than his blond hair and expressive green eyes. Now she felt no attraction, only dread at the prospect of working with a chauvinist pig.

Stan's grin stretched to reveal his dimples. "Sheriff Lexie, we meet again. It's like fate wants us together."

Lexie ignored his outstretched hand. "Or maybe fate is trying to kick me in the butt for some terrible act on my part."

Stan's hand dropped to his side. "Well, that's possible, too."

"Surprised you ended up with the feds," Lexie commented.

"As of last January first, I'm one of the big boys."

The swagger in his voice sharpened Lexie's tongue. "You probably got fired from your detective job in D.C."

"You're quite a comedian. No one fired me. I quit."

A grin played at Lexie's lips, "A woman involved?"

"Are you psychic?"

"I know your history."

"I was thinking about leaving, but left sooner to get out from under my female boss."

Sarah guffawed, "Didn't want her on top, hey?"

Lexie's laugh gurgled out.

"Bedded her once, then she decided I was her private dick. I'm nobody's boy."

"Did you learn anything from the experience, Stan?" Sarah's eyes scrutinized his face.

"I learned that women should back off when a man's had enough."

Lexie shook her head, "You're quite a philosopher."

Sarah switched to detective mode. "This is your fifth month in the Human Trafficking Division?"

"Yes, and I've learned the ropes from the best."

Sarah continued, "Why did they send you south so quickly?"

"This is my territory. My investigation has centered here for the last three months. Most of our evidence is from ads on the Internet and social networking sites. No girls have disappeared from Louisiana, but there was a couple from Alabama, and three each from Mississippi and Georgia in the last month. We think someone is collecting these girls to sell."

"Why haven't you gone after them before this?" Lexie asked.

"Not how it's done. Feds exhaust covert operations first. We collect as much evidence as possible before we close a place down. That way we gather more proof, arrest more people, and then nail them in court."

Lexie broke in, "What's the common factors?"

Thirteen and fourteen-years-old disappeared without a trace near the ocean. Now you see them, now you don't sort of thing. Something is always left behind on the shore. I figure they want us to assume the girls became shark food so we'll stop looking."

"Let's head out," Sarah directed.

As soon as the trio hit the road, Sarah's curious gaze fell on Lexie. "Did you learn anything about Cass and Kent?"

"I got lucky. They were arguing as I circled around to the back of the condo. I waited patiently until Kent left. Cass claimed Kent hugged her and Emma misunderstood. By the way, she attempted to kick me out of the house. I told her she wasn't the one who invited me."

"Do you think one of the pair took Emma?"

"Based on my eavesdropping, I don't think Cass did. She verbally attacked Kent for the possibility that he took Emma.

Of course, that may be a move on her part to make him think she's innocent. Bottom line is neither can be ruled out."

"We'll see," Sarah's tone was dismissive. "Zane's the number one suspect since he left my niece on an empty beach, then lied about it."

Lexie focused out the front window. "Virgil's comments keep running through my mind. You know, what he said about the residents resenting all the rich city folks who take over in the summer months."

Stan spoke up, "So Emma's disappearance is a scare tactic to make the wealthy visitors move elsewhere?"

"Certainly a possibility," Sarah concluded.

Sarah drove past the dive shack to have a shorter walk to the site of Emma's disappearance. The three wandered for an hour looking for anything that resembled a clue.

"Look, Sarah," Lexie pointed to an empty space in a pier board. "Chief Swinson actually sent someone to saw the wood piece with Emma's senior ring."

"That's a shock," Sarah responded.

Forty minutes of searching offered no new insights and the trio returned to the SUV. It was a silent ride toward the condo until Sarah's strained words filled the vehicle interior.

"Lexie, you'll stay elsewhere if Cass is still hot over your accusations."

Lexie felt her face redden.

"Where are you staying, Stan?" Sarah asked.

"It's a cottage near the beach. Do you want to stay with me, Lexie?"

"I'd sooner sleep in the sand."

Within seconds of Sarah parking in front of the condo, Devon appeared on the porch. Lexie held back as Stan and Sarah moved toward him.

Devon's voice was low, but the stillness of the day carried the message to Lexie's ears. "Your sheriff friend isn't welcome here. Cass packed her suitcase, and refuses to have her back in the house."

Sarah growled, "And you're letting her decide?"

"This is her home, too. She said Lexie accused her of hurting Emma. When Cass went in Emma's room she saw that Emma's personal stuff was pilfered by your associate."

"It's an investigation, nephew. We have to know if Emma left clues, secrets, in her personal belongings."

"While she's accusing my wife, and searching Emma's personal things, my daughter is out there going through God knows what." His angry words deteriorated into a mournful wail.

Sarah squeezed his shoulder. "You're right. I'll take care of this." She walked toward Lexie.

Anger invaded Lexie's body.

Sarah reached out the suitcase. "It's better if you stay at the cottages. I'll pay you back for the cost. You work with Stan on the trafficking angle. I'll look closer at Zane and get a handle on any threats against summer residents. I'll meet you two tomorrow at 5 p.m. at the lobster restaurant. We'll pool our findings and see where we're at."

Stan said, "Okay."

Lexie fished the keys out of her purse and headed for the Jeep. The reprimand formed a knot in her gut. She hollered to Stan, "You coming with me?"

"Yes," he jogged to the vehicle.

Lexie felt her jaw stiffen.

Stan grinned, "I'll sprinkle my bottled water on your head to put out the fire."

"You're not funny, Stan. I never thought Sarah was so blind. She has two prime suspects under her nose, and she refuses to acknowledge the possibility of their involvement."

"They're her people. She loves them and doesn't think they'd do bad things. It's human nature."

"Cass isn't her family," Lexie grumbled.

"Maybe Sarah is making you the bad cop, so she can stay in their confidence and in their house."

"That makes sense except for the fact she told me early on to back off her family."

"In view of what came out about Cass and the groundskeeper, I doubt Sarah will ignore them now."

"Regardless, I don't like being her patsy."

"I hear you."

Lexie pointed, "Is that the cottage check-in building?"

Stan pulled a paper from his pocket. "That's it. Rustic Ocean Cottages are economically priced. They even have a toilet, mini fridge, and a microwave according to the advertisement."

"I think that's all I need," Lexie added.

The pleasant woman, at the counter, seemed surprised that the handsome couple requested two cabins.

Each grabbed a bag and walked toward six cottages spaced about eight feet apart. The bright white rentals served as beacons in the night.

Numbers 1 and 2 were assigned to the pair. A small treed area to the west surrounded two white picnic tables, an outdoor grill, and a candy striped swing set.

Lexie was amazed when she unlocked the door and peered into cabin #1. She expected the worse, but the room smelled of sanitizer and looked immaculate. The brown hued floor shined. A red and yellow flowered bedspread coordinated perfectly with the pale yellow walls. A red faux leather chair and a small television took up a third of the room. The last third housed a kitchen cabinet with a stainless steel sink and the promised fridge and microwave.

Everything looked inexpensive, but clean. Lexie dropped her bag on the bed just as Stan appeared at the open door.

"I'm starving. How about I hike up the hill and get dinner to go?" Stan offered.

Lexie managed a smile, "Sounds great."

He asked, "What are you hungry for?"

"Order two of what you're having. I'm not picky."

"I hope it won't take long."

Lexie found a plastic table cover in the cabinet. Two glass plates, plastic forks, and spoons completed her table settings.

She carried everything to a picnic table. A peek of the ocean in the distance offered a bit of a view.

Her thoughts wandered to the first time she met Stan and how attracted she was to him. That was before she found out he was married and a sexist pig. He claimed he was divorced now, but she didn't trust him to tell the truth. However, for some unknown reason, it felt comforting to have him here.

Her anger at Sarah resurfaced. She considered packing and heading home. A woman of her word, she'll follow through on her promised few days. From that point on she'll consider any debt to Sarah paid in full.

Lexie forced Sarah out of her thoughts. The view, the fresh air, and a clean space to stay until she went home were all that mattered at the moment.

"Earth to Lexie," Stan's voice interrupted her thoughts. "Are we having a picnic?"

"That's the plan. The weather's too nice to stay inside."

Stan pulled the covered Styrofoam plates out of a brown paper bag. "Barbeque chicken, fries, rolls and cold slaw," he announced. "Also, a half gallon of turtle ice cream."

Her mind drifted to another picnic, one with bologna and cheese sandwiches. The day Red asked her to marry him and she said 'yes.' That seemed like another life, but she still held out a little hope that someday he'd forgive her.

"I lost you again." Stan's gorgeous green eyes studied Lexie's face.

"Sorry, I was thinking about home." She took a bite of the homemade roll.

"Do you have any insights on this case, Lexie?"

"No thoughts with substance. My second day here and I've already pissed off Chandler and her entire family."

"She's naïve to think her relatives are innocent." Stan swiped a drip of sauce from his chin.

"Why did you show up here so quick, Stan?"

"Because I adore you!" He choked a bit, then continued. "Emma doesn't fit the age range, but we've got a raid in the works so thought I'd check out your case."

Lexie's brows furrowed, "She does fit."

"I thought Sarah's niece was eighteen."

"I'll be right back." Lexie swung her legs over the picnic bench and walked to the cottage then returned.

She handed Stan a photo. "Guess the age of this girl."

"Fourteen?"

"That's Emma Chandler."

Stan rubbed his chin. "She could be one of the victims. She's pretty, built, and looks barely more than a tween."

Lexie stuck the photo in her pocket. "What's the history of your suspects? Where do they find these girls?"

"Theory is they seek out girls near the ocean separated from friends and family. The criminals float away with the girls. No tracks ever found on the beach."

"Did you find personal items from any of them?"

"Always," Stan replied. "As I said earlier, it's like they want us to think the girls drowned. Maybe the traffickers think we'll assume so, and quit looking. Usually a personal item is found stuck under a rock to keep the tide from taking it away."

"That's exactly Emma's circumstance. I found Emma's backpack anchored between two rocks."

"The placements often seemed contrived. My team considers whether or not any given girl drowned or committed suicide."

"Emma's senior ring was wedged into a knot hole in the pier wood. Sarah believed Emma did it to send a message that she didn't drown."

"Any evidence on the ring or the board?"

"I don't know yet. Chief Swinson isn't too motivated to move, much less investigate, from what I've seen."

"First thing in the morning I'll motivate his ass," Stan threatened.

"You'll have to uncork him from his liquor bottle first."

Stan continued, "The bad news is they're stealing girls. The good news is they're still collecting them, which means there's a good chance they haven't left the vicinity for parts unknown. You're smiling?"

"Maybe Emma's still alive. I assumed she was dead."

Darkness ended their conversation. Lexie bagged the remains of dinner. "Do you want ice cream?"

Stan shook his head, "No, I'm full. Got to phone my superior. I'll knock on your door at 7 a.m. How about breakfast, then a visit with Swinson?"

"That works for me. Goodnight."

"Night," he disappeared into cottage #2.

A little surprise and a lot of relief flowed through Lexie's body. She was glad Stan didn't try to seduce her. All she desired was a quiet, alone space.

CHAPTER FOURTEEN

Tye's Case

Tye touched the cell button to stop the noise.

"Wolfe here."

"It's Loretta. I have to talk to you."

"I'm on the way to work. No time for chatter. I have a murder to solve."

"That's what I want to talk about. Come by my house. I don't want to be seen at your office."

"On my way," he replied.

Irritation simmered in his gut. He had no use for Loretta. She cut people to shreds with her sharp tongue. She acted like her fancy house and clothes made her the queen of Diffee. He gripped the steering wheel. *Now she thinks she knows something about my case.*

Tye maneuvered his truck up the winding hill to the two-story house shrouded in pines. Loretta's husband paid big bucks to bring the place back to life after the fire that almost ended the lives of Tye's sister, his wife, Loretta, and another friend, Beth. This morning's fog drifted around the structure giving the illusion of smoke. Tye's chest tightened. He'd almost lost Jamie and Lexie that day—the two most important women in his life. When he exited the truck, he purposely shook his head to ward off the memory.

Her husband's red sports car wasn't in the driveway so this was a private meeting.

The doorbell rang out an unfamiliar tune. Five minutes passed then his fist pounded on the door.

Loretta flung the door open, "Good lord man, grow some patience."

"You called me. What do you want?"

"I want you to stop acting like a grouch. Wipe your shoes before you come in."

He scuffed his boot soles against the welcome pad. *Should be called an unwelcome mat.*

He followed as she moved toward the living room. White carpet, white sofa, white drapes, and lamps on silver toned tables decorated the room. A white grand piano set in the middle of the room. Tye knew for a fact that neither Loretta nor her husband played the piano. Everything projected an image of wealth, not reality.

Loretta sat on the loveseat, her white robe blending into the fabric. "I'd offer you coffee, but I don't allow food or beverages in this room."

Tye sat straight against the hard back of his designated chair and waited. He noted something uncharacteristic in her black-lined eyes—sadness. He'd never known her to be apprehensive about speaking her mind. He forced his voice to civility. "What's going on, Loretta?"

"Our conversation is confidential. It can't get out that I suspect him of killing Wendy. Promise not to tell anyone."

"I don't have to tell anyone. However, if your testimony can convict a criminal, then I'll have to make it known."

"It's speculation based on what happened to me."

"What was that, Loretta?"

"Promise not to tell anyone, especially not your wife?"

"You've got my word." *My promise may turn into a lie, but I want to hear what she thinks she knows.*

"I can't believe I'm confiding in you. Your wife would strangle me for voicing what I'm thinking."

Tye's curiosity peaked. "Jamie knows the possible killer? Is it someone who works with her at the high school?"

"Her father."

Tye leaned forward, "Go on."

"The story about my abortion came out a couple years back. I never named the father. My high school basketball coach, your father-in-law, got me pregnant." Loretta paused, "You don't look shocked."

"Jim's nothing to me, but my wife's father. Why do you suspect him?"

"When I told him about my pregnancy he went crazy. He ordered me to get an abortion. When I told him I wanted to keep the baby his hands wrapped around my throat. 'No way!' he yelled, could I keep his little bastard. The few girlfriends who knew about the pregnancy thought I sacrificed the baby to save my senior year. I actually had the abortion out of fear that Jim would hurt me."

"You think this ties into Wendy's murder?"

"I know it's a stretch, but I thought you should know Jim's past. If he fooled around with Wendy, and she became uncooperative..."

"I get your angle."

"You're the only person I've ever told about Jim."

"I appreciate the heads up. I'll look close at him."

Words fluttered out of Loretta's mouth. "Was Wendy pregnant?"

"No autopsy results have come in. I got to get to work."

Loretta's bitch tone resurfaced. "Remember your promise. Jamie would hate me if this came out, not to mention her mom. Half the town thinks Jim's a coaching saint."

"I hear you."

Tye's head swayed from side to side as he walked toward his truck. *A strange twist.*

His cell beckoned as his truck swerved to follow the downward road.

"Wolfe here."

"Deputy, it's Jason."

"What's up, man?"

"I hung out at the hamburger joint last night. A girl sang 'Hail, Hail the Witch is Dead' out her car window."

"Her name?"

"Starla Jenkins."

"Isn't that one of the girls who pushed Wendy's head in the toilet?"

"Yes, she's the mean one."

"Anything else?"

"No more news today, but I'll stay on it."

"I'll follow up on your report. Thanks, Jason."

Jason might be a good fake deputy, after all.

CHAPTER FIFTEEN

Lexie's Case

Chief Swinson looked too hung over to sit up straight, much less speak, when Stan and Lexie arrived in his office at 8 a.m.

It took a minute for his head to rise from a giant desk calendar. One eye squeaked open and the other eventually followed. "What is it?" he grumbled.

"This is Stan Johnson, a federal agent from Washington D.C. Stan, this is Chief Ted Swinson."

Stan offered a hand to shake, but Ted didn't have enough energy to reach it, so he waved it off. "Unusual to see feds this far south."

The office door swung open, and a young man entered. His uniform matched Swinson's, but his pressed pants and clean shirt gave the opposite impression. Probably in his twenties, but his slicked back red hair, ready smile and freckles made him look sixteen.

Swinson heaved himself up by supporting his palms on the desktop. "I've been here all night, and it's time to head home. Danny will take care of you."

Ted stumbled toward the door.

"He shouldn't drive," Lexie warned.

"He isn't, lives a block down the street. How can I help you folks?"

"I'm here on a federal investigation. My team has intelligence that a sex trafficking gang is operating in the southern states. We think it's time for a raid. Lexie's role here may, or may not, be related."

Lexie picked up on Stan's cue. "Emma Chandler's aunt, a detective in Dallas, asked me to help investigate Emma's disappearance."

"Ah," Danny responded. "I'm working on that. I sent off the wood piece with the ring. It will take a few days to determine if it gives us any useful information. I've interviewed her family and friends. Nothing to report except a rumor that Emma was hot for their groundskeeper, Kent."

Lexie's eyebrows rose. "That's interesting, I heard that Kent and Cass might have something going on."

"Wow, maybe a love triangle," Danny speculated.

"Any of the locals belligerent about the summer people?" Lexie asked.

Danny sat in Ted's vacated chair. "Where'd that idea come from?"

"Man, named Virgil, I met on the beach, said someone might have snatched Emma as a warning to the intrusive summer dwellers."

"Doesn't make sense. Most folks live off summer revenue for the rest of the year. Last thing they want is to run off their profit. Virgil's got an attitude because he's not on the receiving end of any cash."

Stan joined in, "So he's the only one in town who resents the summer crowd?"

"A couple of his buddies join his trash talk. They're no threat as far as I'm concerned. The locals would knock down the sheriff's door if they heard any such rumblings. What's your role in Emma's case, Mr. Johnson?"

"Call me Stan. I'm looking at the sex trafficking angle. My investigation is not specifically related to Emma, but there's a possibility she's one of the kidnapped girls."

Danny frowned, "Hmm."

"I'll give you a heads up if I get enough evidence to make a move."

Danny's voice rippled with enthusiasm. "I'd like to join the operation. I have a lot to learn, and not much opportunity around here."

"I'll keep you informed," Stan promised. "Let's get moving, Sheriff Lexie."

The couple paused outside the door.

"Sucks that Swinson uses that kid as his scapegoat and workhorse. He has potential."

Lexie agreed with a head nod, "Where to?"

"Next comes a three hour round trip to a hunting lodge. Are you up for it."

"What fun," Lexie joked.

"Stay back and listen. This is the beginning of the end for these traffickers. The evidence has mounted and we're about to pull the trigger."

"Hopefully, Emma will get rescued."

"She and many others," Stan replied.

Lexie tossed him the Jeep key. "You drive since you know where we're going."

Settled in the vehicle, they rode quietly for about a mile then he pulled off the highway and answered his phone.

"What's up?" Lexie asked when his call ended.

"I received the go ahead for the raid. You're approved to come along. Are you in?"

"Why wouldn't I?"

"This is dangerous and isn't really your problem."

"It's my problem if Emma is there."

"This sting requires you to play trafficker and work for me. I'm set up to purchase girls. If something goes south, we're both dead."

"Backup?"

"They'll stay at a distance. They hired me so they'd have a new face on the team; someone who wasn't already made as an agent. With the right clothes, I think you'll make a believable thug."

"Thanks for the best compliment you've ever given me."

"If you're in I'll give you the plan on the way. We'll stop at a clothes store to buy heels and an outfit."

"Those for you?"

"Very funny! Are you willing to risk your life today?"

"May I buy red heels?"

"The footwear is your choice."

"Then I'm ready for an adventure."

In the store, Lexie negated the red heels idea as she looked for her trafficker outfit. Stan stood a few feet outside the dressing room swaying his head in a repetitious *no* motion every time she walked out in a new outfit.

Lexie whispered near his ear, "Help, I don't know what's fashionable apparel for someone moving girls into the portals of hell."

Stan fingered through a rack, then pulled a pair of black leather pants off a hanger. He tossed them toward Lexie. Next he selected a leather button front vest to match the pants.

Lexie disappeared behind the dressing room curtain. The pants fit like a second flesh, and the vest was too low cut for her liking.

"Works," Stan stated as she modeled the outfit. "Try on those black boots."

One size smaller and the boots were added to her new persona. "Hair up or down?" she asked.

"Your braid is fine. Let's get on the road." Stan paid and the pair settled back into the Jeep.

"What's the plan?"

"We'll stop at a motel—have wild sex then go to the sting location."

"I'm serious, funny boy, tell me the plan so I won't mess up."

"I suppose you're right, but you look damn hot in leather. I almost bought a whip to match your outfit."

Lexie's words spewed out, "Get serious or I'm gone and my Jeep goes with me. I'll leave your sorry ass on this dirt road."

"Our meeting is at a hunting lodge about seventy miles inland. We're supposed to buy girls for our new operation. My identity as a coordinator has blossomed over the last couple of months. You're my woman."

"For one raid and one raid only," Lexie quipped.

"You're what's called a transporter—the person who actually moves the girls from place to place. There's no reason for you to speak. If they ask you a question, look toward me, or I'll order you to butt out of my business."

"I understand my lowly position."

"We believe the lodge is the front. I'm hoping they'll take us to a back room filled with lost girls."

"You said we have backup?"

"Four agents are in the vicinity."

"Our code word is fiery. If I get knocked out, say I have a fiery temper and agents will knock down the door."

"That's easy enough."

"If you come in direct contact with girls don't ask if they were kidnapped or abused."

Lexie's eyes went blank, "Not sure I understand."

"Some of them are afraid for themselves. Others are told a family member will get hurt or killed if they don't cooperate."

"That makes sense."

"I'm warning you up front that Emma is probably not in this group. She doesn't fit the mold. Girls taken are usually not from wealthy families or white."

"It's worth a try."

Stan stopped the Jeep in a restaurant lot. "We'll get a bite to eat to kill time before our appointment."

Lexie's salad and Stan's steak were ordered and consumed within thirty minutes.

"How about some homemade apple pie?" the waitress offered.

"One for me and one for my woman." Stan winked at Lexie.

The best aroma ever oozed from the pie. Stan spoke between bites. "I never tasted anything this good."

"Delia's pie is better, but this is close."

Stan glanced at his watch, "Time to go, woman."

Lexie followed him like an obedient servant.

CHAPTER SIXTEEN

Tye's Case

Tye pulled to a stop behind the familiar car parked in front of Starla's house. He walked past the vehicle then glanced back. Two teen faces in the car watched him—Lance and a blonde who he assumed was Starla.

What are those two up to?

Tye lifted a hand in greeting, then continued through the broken gate, and across the overgrown yard that ended at the porch. His knock disturbed the spring silence.

A petite blonde woman with a drawn face and baggy eyes opened the door. Cigarette ashes dropped downward as she spoke. "What's up, Deputy?"

"I want your permission to question Starla about Wendy Elliot's murder."

"What for? She didn't have anything to do with that strange girl."

"I heard that Starla harassed Wendy."

"I don't know where she went."

"She's sitting in a car in front of your house with Lance."

The woman sank into a tattered chair. "Not sure if I'll let you question her."

"It's either here or at the sheriff's office."

The woman puffed on the cigarette before her words blasted into a cell phone. "Get in here, Starla."

Tye felt relieved when Lance didn't come in with Starla. He would've sent him packing.

Starla sat her prissy little ass on the sofa in front of Tye. Her features twisted in disgust. She had a lot of attitude for one so young. She looked like a fresher, more confident version of her mother.

"What?"

"What is the question, Starla. What did you do to Wendy Elliot?"

Starla's nostrils puffed, "I didn't get near that weirdo."

Tye fired back, "Already a lie and we just started talking."

"Mom?"

Starla's plea to her mother went unanswered as Dana poked numbers into her cell phone.

Tye continued, "I've heard reports that you harassed Wendy. You pushed her head in a toilet. Also, you called her a witch on your Facebook page."

"That stuff doesn't mean anything. I was joking."

"I'm thinking that a girl who thinks cruelty doesn't matter is a prime murder suspect."

Her mom looked up, "Time for you to go, Deputy. I don't like your accusations."

"Be at my office tomorrow at 10 a.m. Bring an attorney, or not. That's your choice."

He didn't shut the front door when he left. Once on the porch he sidestepped to the left of the screen and listened.

"I ain't got money for an attorney, Starla. You better not be part of that Wendy shit."

"Thanks for the trust, Mom."

"So far there's no evidence that you deserve any."

"If I did kill her, would you even care? You'd probably be too busy with your phone to notice the cops took me away."

"You're such a drama queen."

"I'm just like my mommy."

Their words deteriorated into a clash of screams. Tye jogged to the silence of his truck cab.

Starla could've pulled off the murder by herself. It only took one trigger pull. However, Starla and Lance together was the most likely scenario.

Tye noted the name on the in coming call. Speak of the devil—in this case, think of the devil. "Lance, do you have news on Wendy's case?"

"No one is spilling their guts. Lots of guessing, but no facts."

"What are they guessing?" Tye listened intently.

"Mostly that I'm the guilty one."

"Does it bother you that your friends think you're capable of murder?"

Lance laughed, "I don't have to worry about anyone messing with me."

"Understandable that no one would bully a murder suspect."

"I'll keep trying."

"Thanks for checking in." *I thought he'd come up with wild clues to keep me off his trail, instead he admitted others think he's guilty. That's an unexpected turn of events.*

Tye drove to the high school. As he walked away from his truck, Tye heard Jim chastising the baseball boys for their mediocrity.

"Go home, losers," he hollered.

Tye caught up as Jim tromped toward his office. "You aren't going to have a team much longer if you keep hammering them."

Jim kept moving. "Those slugs don't qualify as a team. What are you doing here?"

"Investigating."

He followed Jim down the steps to the compact office in the basement. Nothing in the office had changed during the last twenty years: same paint, same chair and same three team photos on his desk. Tye's head jerked as he caught sight of the person in Jim's chair—Jamie.

"I thought you were at home."

"I picked up some papers to grade, then dropped by to visit with Dad."

"I need to question him—alone."

"Surely, you're not keeping secrets from your wife." She playfully pinched his arm.

"I'm serious, Jamie. It's confidential."

"I bet Dad will let me listen."

"It's okay with me," Jim chimed in.

Tye's mouth clenched, "It's not okay with me. Leave or I'll waste my time making a second trip here."

Jamie glared at Tye, hugged her dad, then stomped up the stairs.

"You really pissed off my girl."

"Trust me, you don't want her to hear what I have to say."

"Well, get to it."

"I heard a rumor that you seduce teenagers. Was one of them Wendy Elliot?"

"So someone hates me—probably some boy who didn't make one of my teams. They're whispering accusations and you immediately believe them. I always knew you weren't the sharpest pencil in the box."

Anger built in Tye's body. It took all his strength to contain it. "You were interested in her big breasts the first time we talked. That was too personal a comment coming from a teacher. Don't you think?"

"You think I killed her because she wouldn't let me touch her boobs? You make no sense."

"Maybe you killed her because she didn't want to play sex games with you. Did she know one of your dirty secrets?"

"Whoa man, I didn't touch that girl, and she didn't know my secrets. That psychic medium stuff is fool talk."

"I guarantee, if you're responsible for Wendy's death, I'll make sure you pay."

"How do you think your wife will handle you using her father as a scapegoat? You're not smart enough to find the real killer."

The anger on the verge of exploding from Tye's fists, he turned away and mounted the steps.

Outside the building, the wind drained the heat from his body, and dried the sweat-drenched shirt that clung to his back.

That self-righteous son-of-a-bitch impregnated a high school student, and forced Jamie to give away the boys. Bastard.

Confrontation of Jamie's anger filled his thoughts on the too short drive home. Tye heard the boys playing in the backyard. Their voices yelled out a life saving super hero mission.

He headed straight for the kitchen with only one longing glance toward his recliner. It called him to rest prior to his upcoming battle. No time for relaxation. *I'll get the yelling over with before the boys come back in the house.*

Jamie didn't look up. She stirred one pot then stuck biscuits in the oven. Her body language shut him out.

"Let's get this over with Jamie. The silent treatment doesn't help."

"I have nothing to say."

"You're boiling more than the potatoes."

"This issue isn't a joke."

"Your father was accused of seducing a former student."

"Who told you that?" Jamie spouted.

"It's confidential."

"I'm your wife."

"My job requires confidentiality."

Her tone sharpened, "You don't trust me to keep a secret?"

"Usually I do, but this one is too close to home. I don't believe you can be around the accuser without showing your anger."

She slammed the masher on the counter. "Thanks for your vote of confidence."

"I suspect you'd defend your father, regardless. You continue to adore him even though he forced you to adopt out our twins."

"Let it go, Tye. He did it because he thought I was too young and you worthless."

"There you go, still taking up for him."

Jamie waved the gravy spoon, sending sprinkles of liquid onto his shirtfront. "He has the right to confront his accuser."

"I promised to keep the information confidential and I will."

"Is he a murder suspect?"

"Jim's a person of interest."

Seth and Gabriel clamored in the back door.

"Daddy, our rope swing broke," Seth announced.

"It's our airplane today. Come on, Daddy." Gabriel pulled him toward the door. "We can't save the world without it."

Tye gave his boys hugs then followed them out the door. *They did save someone—Daddy from Mommy.*

CHAPTER SEVENTEEN

Lexie's Case

Stan glanced at the map. They followed a two lane paved road that ended with a line of orange cones. He came to a quick stop, backed up, then took the rocky terrain around the cones.

Lexie gripped the armrest.

Stan spoke above the clatter, "Your Jeep's out of alignment."

"Not until you became the driver."

They arrived at their destination after a bumpy, rock-spitting ride. A log lodge set in the middle of nowhere.

Two guards stood on the porch guzzling beers and shooting the breeze. One man held a rifle, the other a pistol.

Pistol packer's hand lingered near his weapon. "What's your business?"

Stan's tone hardened, "I'm Stan Dearing. I've got business with Aaron Belford."

"Wait here while I check it out."

Pistol opened the door and bellowed, "Dearing here."

A voice called, "Send him back."

It looked like a traditional hunting lodge lobby. The furniture was all pine. Cushions decorated in animal prints were tossed on leather furniture. A deer head was situated in the middle of a giant stone fireplace. Heads of smaller animals surrounded the antlered mounting.

A woman sat at a desk with a welcome sign on its surface. A bespectacled man leaned on the desk. Lexie figured he was in his late forties. A solid brown bowtie matched the stripe in his shirt. He looked like a math teacher.

Stan reached out a hand, "Aaron?"

"Of course, Mr. Dearing. Who is your lovely companion?"

"Lexie—my woman and partner."

"Pleased," he petted her outreached hand.

Hairs stood up on Lexie's arms.

Their butts barely hit the chair seats in Belford's office when his phone rang.

"Of course," he said, "Thank you."

Lexie noted the clench in Belford's jaw.

"It appears, Stan, that there's a flaw in our business proceedings."

Stan's body stiffened, "We have a deal. I have customers to satisfy."

"You're a liar, Stan."

He blasted out, "What are you talking about?"

"My man said your vehicle has an Oklahoma tag. Strange for a man from Las Vegas."

"My tag has nothing to do with our business."

"A liar is a liar."

"It's another method to keep my anonymity. I didn't want anyone tracking me by my state tag, so I used the Jeep."

"Did you pick up the lady sheriff for cover, too?"

Stan's face paled.

"Her pretty face was on the cover of the local paper a couple of years back when she nabbed that serial killer."

"You're mistaken," Stan didn't move.

Belford walked to the door, and swung it open, "OUT!"

"My associates will hear how you backed out on our deal. They'll cut off your fingers instead of mine."

"Whatever," Belford replied. His eyes turned to Lexie, "Nice meeting you, honey."

Lexie focused on the floor as she followed Stan out. His long, stiff strides moved toward the Jeep. Inside, his fists beat the wheel, "Damn him to hell."

A voice came on the listening device.

"Son-of-a-bitch Stan! You fucked the operation by bringing in a woman and her personal vehicle. We'll meet you at the orange cones to pick up the transaction money."

Lexie noted the scowl on Stan's face, but decided to speak anyway. "You said you got permission for me to ride along."

"I lied."

Lexie sat silently, No point in poking an infuriated bear.

As soon as they arrived at the cones, a large man with a face contorted by anger appeared at the Jeep window. Stan reached the bag of money toward his boss.

Spit sprayed out with his words. "You're fired, Fool! Report at 8 a.m. Tuesday to get your last check and turn in your badge."

Cuss words sizzled from Stan's mouth as he sped off.

"Let's drive around a few minutes," Lexie proposed. "It's logical that the girls are housed close to the lodge."

Stan's tone was controlled. "True. Transporting loads of girls in and out from a distance might arise suspicions."

"On the way to the lodge I saw a side road that was travel worn. Might as well see where that road will take us," Lexie suggested.

"I'll pull out of sight until my former co-workers pass by, then we'll circle back toward the lodge."

The pair waited three or four minutes before the official vehicles sped by leaving a cloud of dust above Lexie's hidden Jeep.

"Let's head out," Stan directed.

"There's the road. I almost missed it in the dark." Lexie pointed. "I see a light in the distance."

Two to three miles later Stan pulled off the road into a treed area. Lexie secured flashlights from the glove compartment. Their feet tromped through weeds and dead branches toward a lone light. A full moon guided their way.

The light shone from within a black two-story house that hid behind a circle of trees. The moon's glow reflected off an eight-foot security gate. The six-foot fence that surrounded the place was a quicker climb. Lexie raised a foot to start up.

"Stop," Stan hissed into the night. "It may be electrified."

"Thanks," she murmured.

Stan threw a rock at the top of the enclosure. No sparks sprinkled into the darkness.

Lexie placed her hands on the barbwire fence, the cold points pierced into her palms. She pulled herself to the next string of wire. The continued poking brought dots of blood to her palms and fingers. She reached the top and swung a leg over. Balance lost, she grabbed the top of the wire fence impaling her hands into metal points. She screeched, then fear gripped her as she realized an adversary might have heard."

"You okay?" Stan called from below.

She felt blood trickling down her arms as she pulled her hands slowly from the pointed wire. Unable to tolerate the pain, she jumped. One foot caught in the fence and she hung suspended above the ground.

"Hang on," Stan yelped. He was up and over the fence in a flash. He held Lexie's upper body as she pulled out her foot. His bloody hands balanced her body as she struggled to stand upright.

"Thanks—again," she whispered.

Stan led the way as they did a combination run-crawl on a random path toward the structure.

Under the window, Lexie slowly rose to peek in. A man caught her eyes.

"Go," she shoved Stan. "He saw me."

The front door slammed and running feet came toward her.

She moved toward the sound. A hairy-faced man waved a rifle in the air a few feet from her face.

CHAPTER EIGHTEEN

Lexie's Case

"Sorry, for sneaking around," Lexie uttered. "I didn't think anyone lived here. My car broke down and I was looking for shelter.

He grabbed her upper arm and yanked. "That's crap, girl!"

Hairy slung her forward as they entered the house. Lexie lay on the hardwood floor at his feet.

"Belford told me to watch out for a couple nosing around our operation. Where's your partner?"

"Out in the dark, waiting for the opportunity to shoot you in the head. You might want to stay away from the windows."

"Cops can't kill without a reason."

"We're not cops. We're private detectives. We don't lose our jobs if we kill someone who's trying to kill us. I assume you're a guard, not a murderer?"

"Why are you sneaking around here?"

"We're looking for a blonde teenager named Emma. She disappeared a few days ago off the coast. Her rich daddy wants her back. Is she here?"

"Ain't got no girls. You're making up shit."

Lexie pulled the phone out of her pocket.

His foot kicked her leg. "Put that down."

"I want to show you something." Lexie searched Emma Chandler's name on the Internet, then handed the phone to Hairy. "There's the story. See her dad is a bigwig. He's offering a fifteen thousand dollar reward for information leading to her recovery."

"What's that got to do with me?"

"Me and my partner will get a big payoff. I'll share a couple of bills if you're willing to help."

"You don't care about any other girls?"

"Hell no—only one that matters is the one with a rich daddy. You can buy lots of good booze with that money."

"Belford will have me shot in the head."

"Tell him she ran off. He's won't report anything. You can leave and find a place that's not isolated. You look like a man who loves the ladies."

"You got cash?"

Lexie punched numbers into her cell phone. "Stan, I found a guy who's willing to sale us our girl for two thousand."

"Four," burst out of Hairy's mouth.

Lexie's words shot back, "Don't screw with me man. We already made a deal."

"I think I deserve half. I got the girl, and you got nothin'.

Lexie grumbled into the phone, "You hear that? Now he wants half for finding Emma. I shouldn't have told him about her rich daddy. Now he's turned greedy."

The line went silent for a few seconds. "Offer a third."

"Damn it, Stan, a third is too much for a stranger."

"I'll take it," Hairy yelped.

"You get the cash, Stan. I'll stay here so he'll know we're on the up and up. I'll ask him to deactivate the gate so you can get out."

Hairy sat a few feet away on a tattered sofa gawking at a television. A trickle of tobacco dripped from his chin. He brushed it away with his shirtsleeve. Lexie wanted to bash him in the head and search for Emma, but she knew better than to risk it.

The clock ticked beside her. This was taking too long. Even dull Hairy was likely to get suspicious. She hoped Stan wasn't having difficulty-convincing Boss to give him the money. Fifteen more minutes passed, then an hour and still no Stan.

The show ended. Hairy walked toward Lexie. One hand fisted her braid, then he jerked her against his body. "Where the hell is he? Next shift starts in less than an hour. I can't go through with this if my replacement shows up. He'll either squawk to Belford or we'll have to share the loot."

"We hid the Jeep. I'm afraid my partner had trouble finding it."

"He better show soon or the deal's off. I'll take you to Belford. He'll think I'm the best employee he ever had and give me a reward."

"You think Belford will hand over a $5,000.00 bonus? You don't look like a fool."

Pounding on the door overrode the television volume.

Hairy leveled his shotgun, "Let him in."

Lexie opened the door, "It's about time you got here. I thought you took off without me."

"I'd leave you sugar, but not a little bitch worth fifteen thousand bucks."

Lexie fisted and clobbered Stan's shoulder. "You're a hateful piece of shit."

"Can't live on love," Stan snorted. "Ain't that right, mister?"

"Hell, yes," Hairy spit a stream of chew into the fireplace.

Stan fisted a brown paper bag, "Here's your take."

Hairy looked inside, "Ain't got time to count, but if it's not all here I'll find you and gut you."

"It's all there," Stan assured him.

Hairy pulled a ring of keys from his pocket. The pair followed him toward a basement door. He unlocked it, then waited at the top with his rifle.

Uneasiness gripped Lexie. If this was a trick: they were trapped.

The dark space smelled of urine and feces. A pot set beside the stairwell.

Their entry brought the girls to sitting on dirty mats. Two Hispanic girls, four African-Americans and two white girls all scantily dressed in bras and panties were housed in the filthy space. Lexie studied their faces.

Lexie pointed, "That's her. Come on, sister, you're coming with us."

The teen smoothed her hair and quickly pulled on old jeans and a T-shirt.

"Hurry," Hairy ordered from the top. "This is taking too long."

The three climbed the steps.

"You said your girl was blonde."

Lexie responded, "Someone dyed her hair to hide her identity."

Stan led the way as Hairy eyeballed them across the front yard. Stan slowed beside her. "We'll run toward the Jeep. As soon as we hit a blind spot I'll turn back. The thug will open the gate. That'll give enough time for my team to get through. Stay out of sight. I'll find you when it's over."

Lexie grabbed the girl's hand and ran: the teenager stumbled. Lexie knelt down, "Get on my back." The girl gripped her shoulders, then wrapped her legs around. Several steps later Lexie's heart raced. "Slide off and lie flat. I hear a car coming."

"I'll be good," she whimpered. "Don't kill my mommy."

"What's your name?"

"Kylie," she whispered.

"Where do you live?"

"Mississippi," she stuttered.

"Kylie, I'm a sheriff and soon you'll go home. The man with me is Stan. He'll save the other girls."

Kylie wrapped her arms around Lexie. Sobs heaved out of the girl's mouth. *No Emma, but one girl will go home if the raid blows up.*

Lexie heard the squeal of the metal gate opening, then the black SUV slipped through. Five minutes later she heard a shot ring out. Another five minutes and an old truck sent rocks flying in all directions. Panic gripped her. Stan didn't know Hairy's backup was due to arrive. *Would they be so involved with the girls they wouldn't be on alert?*

"That's your captor's partner." I must warn the agents."

"No," Kylie squeaked.

"Stay in the bushes." Lexie pulled a blanket from her back seat. "Wrap this around you."

Lexie stayed in the shadows of the trees as she ran forward. She peered into the same window that caused her prior capture. Hairy's body lay still on the floor. The broad back of a man stood in front of Stan and three agents. *Shoot him in the back?*

"You guys are dead meat." The shooter promised as he leveled his weapon.

The window shattered as Lexie's bullet hit the glass. The man fell face forward onto the wood floor. She circled the house to the front door.

Stan's boss hollered, "Damn it, gal. You saved us!"

Lexie shivered at the sight of the stranger's bloody head. "I got to get back to Kylie."

"I'm right behind you," Stan called.

"We've got work to do, Johnson. Let her get the girl," Boss ordered.

"Do it yourself: I'm fired." He trotted to catch up with Lexie.

She slowed, "I think you'll be unfired if you stay."

"Five months was long enough with that jerk. I'm ready to move on."

They found Kylie crying uncontrollably under the blanket.

"She has to be processed with the other girls."

"I'm not sure she can handle it," Lexie replied.

"There's no choice. I'll walk her back to the door."

Stan took Kylie's hand and led her back to the cabin. Lexie saw Kylie clinging to Stan on the front porch. A sorrowful screech of a repetitive "no" filled the air.

"One of the girls," he said, when Boss came to the door.

"Get to work, Stan. Help us gather evidence. After all, this was your bust." Boss continued, "I don't think that little gal will turn loose of you anytime soon."

Kylie's hand stayed locked in Stan's as he walked toward the Jeep window. "I'll finish here and make sure the girls get home safely. Thanks for saving my life. There'll be questions for you to answer. Tonight we'll gather evidence and interview the girls. Head back to the cottage. I know where to find you when it's your turn to give a statement."

"Okay. It's been a long day. Goodbye, Kylie. The nightmare is over."

She clung tighter to Stan.

"Sorry Emma wasn't here," Stan empathized.

"Eight girls were saved. That's a good day."

The clouds covered the moon as Lexie drove through the darkness. Her headlights searched the road for the way to the cottages.

I should be happy, but it's difficult when the one girl I wanted to find is still gone without a trace.

CHAPTER NINETEEN

Tye's Case

The morning drizzle fit Tye's mood. He purposely left early to avoid Jamie. He picked up a sausage biscuit, tater tots and coffee at the restaurant then drove toward Mud Creek. After driving a few miles out of town the environment offered solace and peace. The recent rain left a shine on nature. The vibrant green landscape against the clear water looked like a fantasy scene.

Tye walked to the shore, paper bag in hand, then settled to dine on the earth's table. Birds chirped, a snake slithered by, but all his awareness focused on Wendy's murder and the lack of evidence.

The cell phone interrupted his self-doubt session. "What's up, Sis? Have you found Emma?"

"Bust last night was a bust for me. Eight girls were rescued, but no Emma. I'm as lost as if it was day one. Is there any new information regarding Wendy's case?"

"There's no solid evidence. Lance and Starla are at the top of my suspect list. My father-in-law is a person of interest. Apparently, Jim has a thing for teenage girls."

"Oh no!"

"Oh yes! Jamie's not talking to me. She doesn't believe her old man could harm a kid. I'll follow up on Wendy's autopsy report this afternoon."

"I planned on driving home today, but Sarah's superior had a stroke. She hurried back to Dallas. She was mad as a wet hornet because Stan and I didn't show for her scheduled meeting at a restaurant. In spite of her nasty attitude, I agreed to stay two more days to follow-up on her leads."

"So we're both in the same place—nowhere," Tye summarized.

"At least you know where Wendy is. Emma vanished without a trace."

"Do you think she's dead?"

"There's been no ransom demand, and a lot of time has passed since her disappearance. My best hope, other than the trafficking angle, was that someone took her to get a payoff, which is no longer feasible. To answer your question, I do think she's dead."

"Time for me to move on down the road, Sis. Bradford is supposed to have an attendance report ready from the day Wendy went missing. Soon I'll find out who besides Wendy didn't show up for afternoon classes on her murder day."

"Good luck, Bro."

"Same to you, Sis."

Tye dropped his breakfast trash in the can, then headed toward Diffee High.

The school was alive with young bodies when Tye entered the building. Bradford's secretary waved a list in the air as soon as he opened the office door. "Here's what you wanted. Mr. Bradford said to tell you about the Senior Awards Assembly the hour after lunch on the day that Wendy died. It's impossible to know who was and wasn't there in such a big group."

Tye rubbed his forehead. More bad news, the killer had extra time to get back to class after the murder. Scary to imagine a teenager so cold blooded he murdered Wendy, then returned to solve math equations or diagram a sentence.

Tye took the paper then sat on a metal fold-up chair. He eyeballed the names on the list of absentees. Rick, the longhaired baseball player, and Starla were both on the list. Lance's name wasn't there, which meant he was in class that afternoon.

Tye walked into the lobby and visually screened faces.

"Hey, Rick." He shouted toward a guy hurrying through the front door.

Rick startled. He caught sight of Tye's summoning hand.

"What's up, Deputy?"

"Your name is on this list of kids who didn't return to class Thursday afternoon. You probably recall that was the same day Wendy died."

"Talk to my folks."

"I doubt they can tell me why you skipped classes the same afternoon someone murdered Wendy."

Rick fingered his ear. "I... I didn't study for my semester English test. I skipped out thinking I'd make it up in a few days."

"Where did you go?"

"I hung out around the park until time to go home."

Tye couldn't read the kid's eyes because he focused on the floor. "Did anyone see you there?"

"That was the last thing I wanted to happen."

"Too bad you don't have a witness, considering the situation. Did Wendy ever nose into your personal life?"

"She never bothered me. I liked her, but kept my distance. The guys would've given me hell if I admitted it."

"Bravery is obviously not one of your strong points."

"Can I go? The bell is about to ring."

"Go."

Bradford called across the lobby. "Any news, Tye?"

"I don't have any solid evidence. I've got to get back to my office for a meeting at ten."

"Keep me informed."

"I will, Mr. Bradford."

Tye's curiosity peaked as he drove toward his office. Will Starla show up with an attorney? If she doesn't, is that an indication of innocence? In Starla's case, it'll probably mean her mom doesn't have money to pay for legal assistance.

The office door slammed into Tye's belly as he reached for the handle. Delia's tear-filled eyes lowered as she shuffled out. "Delia, what's wrong?"

She shook her head and walked across the street to Dixie's restaurant.

Tye's eyes met his mother's. "What are you doing here?"

Her bottom lip protruded in a fake pout. "I'm not allowed to visit my son?"

"You don't usually show up at my work."

"I was catching up with Delia."

"What exactly did you say to her?"

"We talked about a variety of things. She'd be attractive if she'd lose that fat. I can only imagine how much she must eat to maintain that weight. I told her about a diet pill some of my overweight friends like."

"What else?"

"I don't like the tone of your voice."

"Delia was upset."

"She's been mad for years because I took Cecil away from her—twice. Margo's blue eyes twinkled. Her red lips stretched into a smile. I wish she'd like me long enough to fix me up with that good looking friend of hers."

"Delia and Sloan are a couple," he said firmly.

Margo fluffed her hair. "You're kidding?"

He snapped back, "I'm serious."

"What does he see in her? The world is a crazy place."

""Delia is a kind, hardworking woman."

"Son, you know nothing about relationships. You've kept Jamie since high school. If you looked around, you could've found a feminine classy woman like Loretta."

"Time to leave, I have people coming in for questioning."

"You and Lexie are always playing cops. I'd be bored to death."

Delia followed the mother and daughter in the door.

Margo winked at Delia as she exited. "Don't forget what I told you."

Tye noted the puffy redness under Delia's eyes. Lexie would've known how to comfort her. He didn't know, and didn't want to learn, how to deal with female dramatics.

Tye motioned Starla and her mom to the six-foot white plastic table that served as a cheap conference area. Tye sat on one side facing the mother and daughter.

"Delia, please take notes."

She pulled a pad from her desk and sat on a chair beside him.

Dana's question burst out, "Are you charging my daughter?"

"Depends on what she has to say for herself."

"Can I stop the questioning?"

"If, at any point, you want an attorney present, we'll stop."

"Okay," Dana agreed.

"My first question, Starla, is why did you attempt to drown Wendy in a school toilet?"

Venom mixed with her answer, "I wanted to scare her."

"You admit you did it. Why did Cara take part?"

"She's my best friend. We have each other's backs."

"Was it your idea to drown Wendy?"

"I put Wendy's shit flowing mouth in the toilet where it belonged."

The color faded from Dana's cheeks.

"What shit are you talking about, Starla?"

"She told me to stay away from Lance. Said his dead daddy didn't like me. She thought her ghost story would scare me off. I knew what she was up to. She had a crush on Lance."

"According to the school attendance record, you skipped out the afternoon Wendy died."

Dana broke in, "Where were you?"

"Home in bed. Sick."

"You never mentioned that before now."

"Like you'd care," Starla snapped.

Tye ground his stare into her face. "You better have a witness girl, or you're in way deep."

Her words blurted out, "Rick took me to the house."

"Did he stay with you?"

"We were together all afternoon."

Dana's tone hardened, "Did you have sex with that boy?"

"Don't be a prude, Mother. At least I have proof I didn't kill the witch."

Confusion echoed through Dana's words. "You told me you loved Lance."

"He's all 'let's wait—make sure we're right for each other.' Just because he's waiting doesn't mean I can't go at it with someone else."

Dana pulled a tissue from her purse and blotted her face.

"Starla, you have a problem. Rick claimed he was alone that afternoon."

"Duh, Rick and Lance are best friends. He won't admit he screwed Lance's girl."

"Why would Rick have sex with his best friend's steady?"

"It was exciting to sneak around. Lance trusted us both. He never suspected a thing."

"We'll see if your game was worth it when Lance finds out his best friend and his girl are cheats and worse."

"We don't plan on telling anyone."

Tye flat handed the top of the table. "Then you've got quite a dilemma. Without a witness to verify where you were that afternoon, you're my number one murder suspect."

"That's ridiculous. I'm a teenage girl."

"It doesn't take much strength, or sense, to fire a gun. Maybe you didn't mean to kill her? Charges are less if it wasn't premeditated murder."

Dana's hands grasped each other.

Starla's smirk turned to fear. "You really think I did it?"

"At this point, you're the only possibility. I want someone locked up. The public doesn't like the idea of a murderer running lose in the county, and it hurts my reputation."

Starla punched numbers into her cell phone. "Rick, tell the truth. Deputy Wolfe thinks I killed Wendy. I don't give a damn what Lance thinks about us doing it. You help me, or I'll make sure you never get any again."

Tye took the phone Starla reached toward him. Nervous words jittered into Tye's ear. "Starla and I stayed together from about noon to 4 p.m. Does Lance have to know about this?"

"You better tell him before I do. Lance deserves to know you aren't a true friend."

The call finished. Tye turned back to Starla. "You're not home free. I heard how you put words in Rick's mouth. Don't sleep too sound tonight. If another suspect doesn't show up, you'll stay at the top of my list."

"You can take your daughter home. Don't leave the county," Tye warned.

Dana wrapped her arm around her daughter's shoulder as they exited. Starla shrugged it off.

"That girl sure has a mean streak," Delia said. "A warning to young men should be posted on her back."

The backdoor rattle announced Brody and Adam's entrance.

Tye acknowledged his sons, "What's up, guys?"

"We came by to show you my new art." Adam revealed a tattoo on his shoulder.

"Is that snake identical to your brother's?"

"Almost. My snake has blue eyes, and his black."

"He wasn't man enough to have blood dropping from his snake's eyes," Brody teased.

"Too creepy for me," Adam countered.

Delia put on her glasses and looked closely at the snake that curved down Adam's back. "Well, hmm."

Brody moved toward the door. "We got to head out. I'm going to church with Myrna tonight."

"Goodbye, guys."

"I can't believe how much your boys look alike."

"Adam was skinny and Brody muscular. Now they work out together, and Adam's muscles have about caught up. I'm afraid I won't be able to tell them apart before long."

Delia didn't hide the surprise in her voice. "Your hell raiser started to church?"

"Yep, that's something I never expected to see—Brody a church goer."

"He's come a long way since he first moved to Diffee," Delia said.

"I hate to admit it, but I didn't think there was a chance he'd become a decent man. I'm glad to eat my words."

The FAX machine's hum filled the office. Tye retrieved the county coroner's report when it dropped from the machine.

He read to Delia. "Wendy's killer shot her in the chest, at close range, using a 45 caliber pistol. All the other marks on her body were attributed to the tornado's fury."

He silently scanned the rest of the report looking for what he most wanted to know. Finally, he found it. "Wendy wasn't raped or pregnant—a virgin."

The report didn't prove his father-in-law innocent, but likely he wasn't the murderer. Which was good for Tye's marriage. It also ruled out someone attacking Wendy for sex. That supported the conclusion that the killer wasn't a stranger.

Delia reached the phone toward him. "It's Jason."

"Have you found out anything?" Tye asked the teen.

"I haven't got any news. I heard Starla was in your office today. Did you arrest her?"

"There isn't enough evidence to charge her."

"Oh," disappointment breathed out with his words. "I thought she did it."

"We'll keep looking."

"I should've told you sooner, but I was so sure Lance or Starla killed Wendy that I didn't mention it."

"Mention what?"

"Mr. Moore, our bus driver, had a thing for Wendy. Patted her back sometimes. Once I saw him slip her a hundred dollar bill."

"Did you ask Wendy about Moore?"

"She called me 'jealous' and refused to answer my questions."

"I'll look into it, Jason. Call me tomorrow."

With Jason's words, Starla dropped to suspect number two in Tye's brain. Bus driver Trey Moore became the frontrunner. Easy for him to kill Wendy, then return her body to the stadium after his bus route.

CHAPTER TWENTY

Lexie's Case

Lexie's day started with a short goodbye to Sarah, and a quick conversation with Tye. That followed by a drive to the scene of the raid to answer questions and describe her actions. A voice hollered as soon as her left foot stepped in the door.

"Stay out! I don't want another DNA sample in the mix."

Lexie looked at the agent's nametag. "Too late, Fred. My DNA is already here. I participated in the raid last night."

Boss spoke up, "Yes, she saved my ass. You can decide whether you want to thank her later, or not at all."

Fred chuckled, "That decision will take a few days."

"Head to the basement," Boss directed, "I need answers."

Lexie slowed as she reached the bottom step. "Why are you here, Danny?"

A smile stretched his face, "I get to help."

You'd have thought Danny was invited to the celebrity suite at the Super Bowl.

"I'm learning lots of stuff. We've collected DNA from everything, even inside the vehicles. We bagged all the girl's clothes. Boss said we couldn't let the girls wear paper overalls because that wasn't good psychology. I bought some clothes for them at the thrift shop in town. Agents took photos of the girls in their own clothes on the mats. Then photos were shot of locks on the doors. Bruises and sores were also photographed. Sometimes the girls lie out of fear, but eventually they come to trust us if we treat them with respect." Danny finally ran out of verbal momentum.

"Where's Stan?" Lexie asked.

"He's working the lodge site," Boss answered. "The place has twenty cabins and fifteen rooms we've got to get samples from. Not to mention DNA samples from all the employees."

Danny's enthusiasm surfaced again. "It's cool. The agents cross-check the DNA from the lodge site with the holding site to prove those folks are connected with the kidnappings."

Lexie's eyes scanned the room, "Where are the girls?"

"They had medical exams and we took statements, then we moved them to a safe house. Couple of them didn't speak English, so we're waiting for an interpreter to question them," Boss informed.

Lexie sat at a card table. "Sounds like quite an operation."

"It's a huge effort," Boss remarked. "With regular crimes law enforcement usually has one location, one victim, and one perpetrator. In sex trafficking cases those numbers can run in the hundreds."

Lexie shook her head. "I don't want your job."

A male voice boomed from above, "Where's my girl?"

"Hang back, man," Fred's voice ordered. "This is a crime scene."

"Give me my daughter. I heard on the news that eight girls were rescued. Where's my Misty?"

Boss raced up the steps as the man's words heated. Lexie followed.

"I'll take care of this, Fred. How can I help you, sir?"

"My daughter, Misty Rose, disappeared the last week of March. I've come to take her home."

"Do you have a photo?"

"Not on me," the man squealed.

Lexie intervened, "Did you get a call your daughter was found?"

"No, but she must be here."

Boss's expression clouded. "How old is your daughter? What does she look like?"

"She's seventeen, five foot-eight inches, slim, and has dark hair."

"I'm sorry, sir, that doesn't fit the description of any of the found girls. All of them are less than five-five. The oldest girl in the group is fourteen."

"YOU'RE WRONG! She's here. Her mom won't stop crying. I can't bear it anymore. I promised to bring Misty home."

Boss's words were firm, "Misty isn't here."

The man's body slumped, his eyes still, he walked out the door as if in a trance.

"What a horror story, never knowing if your child is alive or dead. I don't think he can bear much more," Lexie worried.

"He's about over the edge," Boss agreed.

"Do you think there's another group of girls hidden somewhere? That would explain what happened to Emma and Misty."

Boss tugged as his chin. "No doubt there are many hidden girls, but those two don't fit the age range. Also, Misty's height is taller than the girls they steal. The sickos want to rape females that look like little girls, not women. But I never say never."

Sorrow tightened Lexie's chest. "I don't know if it's bad news or good that they don't have Emma. If traffickers have her, she's still alive."

"Let's sit at the kitchen table, so I can take your statement."

Lexie answered questions and retraced her movements for a tedious three hours. Finally, she reached the point where she falsely identified Kylie as Emma to rescue her.

Boss's face twisted in disgust. "You and Stan are quite a pair. You two screwed up the meeting with Belford. Now you're telling me you took Kylie from the scene. Some lawyer can claim that Kylie wasn't in the house, and it was you who transferred material to her. You're not supposed to remove a victim from the scene before she's examined."

"I thought saving one child was better than none."

"You got a lot to learn," he growled.

Lexie's chair slammed to the floor as she scrambled to her feet. "As you noted earlier, I saved your ass. If I didn't rescue you, Kylie would've been the only girl saved. It's probably not procedure for you to stand in front of a gunman with your hands on your head, but it happened. I'm out of here before you throw another tantrum."

Lexie caught Fred's nod as she sped out the door.

·····•••●●•••·····

When she reached the cottage, she tossed the keys on the kitchen table. Then changed into blue jean shorts and a white T-shirt.

She walked to the restaurant for chicken and sides for two. Then she returned to the cottage to wait, and wait, and wait some more for Stan's arrival.

At 8 p.m. she ate her share of the meal and stuck Stan's back in the fridge. She didn't have a clue what time or if he'd return to his cottage tonight. He probably already ate, but she'd keep watch anyway. Finally, she roosted on the porch swing. Around 9:30 p.m. a government car braked in front of Stan's rental. He walked forward, shoulders slumped, head down.

"Hungry?" Lexie called.

"I'm starved, but too tired to walk up the hill."

"I'll warm up the chicken I bought earlier."

"You're an angel."

Lexie laughed, "That's me!"

"I'll take a quick shower. I analyzed scum all day."

Lexie spooned Stan's dinner onto a glass plate. She spread a cloth over the table, and started to put a candle in the middle. She stopped and pushed the cloth and candle back in the cabinet. Confusion clouded her thoughts. *Why did I keep wandering around waiting for Stan? A candle on the table? Geez, seems like I'm setting up a seduction. What am I doing?*

Lexie scraped his chicken, mashed potatoes, gravy, and slaw from the plate back into the restaurant's Styrofoam container.

Ten minutes later he called through her open door. "Food, food before I pass out."

"Your feast," her hand waved him toward the table.

She sat opposite him—silent.

"Talk to me woman. I just want to chew."

"Nothing new to report. All paths to Emma led nowhere. I put all my hope on the trafficking angle. Sarah's taken off and expects me to follow up on loose ends with Zane, and any mad residents. By the way, Chief Swinson called a community meeting for tomorrow afternoon. I have no idea what he's up to."

Stan paused between bites. "I'm leaving in the morning. Will you take me to the airport?"

"After I drop you off I'll attend the meeting to find out what Swinson's so secret about, then head home. Nothing left for me to do here."

"No clues, no case," Stan acknowledged. "Where's that turtle ice cream?"

"I'll find it for you."

"Let's eat on the porch. I was shut in all day. Fresh air might clear my head."

Lexie pulled out two spoons, then retrieved dessert from the fridge.

The pair sat on the porch, their legs dangling off the edge.

Stan licked the spoon. "Chocolate, nuts, and caramel on vanilla ice cream—food for the gods."

A spoonful of ice cream fell from her spoon. Stan took her hand and licked the chunk off.

A wave of passion flooded Lexie's body. "You really are hungry."

"Sexually."

The night hid her reddening face. Her spoon quivered as she dug it into the ice cream.

His hand pressed over hers. "I feel bad that I didn't help you find Emma."

"It was well worth the try since you saved eight others."

"We saved," he corrected. "Let's work out your frustrations in bed."

"Sex won't cure my ills."

"We can keep at it until you stabilize."

"You're quite a temptation, Stan, but I'm still hung up on my ex fiancé."

"He'll never know. I want sex, not commitment," Stan spouted.

"You seemed different this time, changed, but you're still the same ass chaser."

"I am who I am. Take it or leave it."

Lexie stood, then paused as she touched the doorknob. "Watch carefully, I left it!"

Lexie showered and crawled into bed. Her arms squeezed a pillow against her fetal positioned body. You never know if a man will stay or go. A pillow, however, was always available to hug. *I'm glad Stan returned to his usual asshole self before I fell in bed with him.* Her eyelids closed.

····•••●●•••····

Lexie startled awake. The shadow of a man loomed at the side window. She rolled to the floor. A rapid knock rattled the pane. She crawled to the side of the window and stood.

"Lexie," Stan's voice was low and raspy. "Open the window."

She twisted the lock then pushed open the window. "What do you want?"

"Not what you think."

"Now that you've lost your job you can become a comedian." Lexie pushed the window downward.

Stan's hands braced at the bottom and pushed up. "Listen."

"I'm not interested in anything that comes out of your mouth."

"You're interested in this."

"So tell me."

His head stuck through the open window. "Cass is entertaining in cottage #3. She's with a slender, longhaired, muscular man. Does that fit the description of the hired help you heard Cass hugged?"

"Exactly."

"Are you sure it's her?"

"The guy called her Cass. He told her to hurry before someone saw her. They just went in so they'll probably go at it for a while. What's our next move, Sheriff Lexie?"

"Let me think. Are they inside now? If so, come in the front door."

"I'll check."

Lexie opened the front door, then sat on a kitchen chair. Stan's eyes crawled over every curve of her body that was barely covered by bikini nighties.

"I'll be right back." She slipped into the bathroom and put on yesterdays dirty clothes.

"I preferred the natural look. Now that I know what I'm missing, I'm depressed."

"Don't distract me. I must think about alternatives."

Stan's jaw tightened, "Yes, your majesty."

Lexie studied the problem with head in hands. She looked up, "I'm phoning Devon."

"Are you sure that's a good idea?"

"He needs to know what kind of woman he married. Maybe then he'll consider her and Kent suspects."

Stan cheered, "Go for it."

A little apprehension was mixed with excitement as she poked in the phone number.

Devon's nervous voice rang out, "Did you find Emma?"

"No, but I have a lead in her case."

"Where are you?" he asked.

"I'm at Rustic Cottages in #1. Don't drive in front of the cottages. Park in the lot by the restaurant, then walk down."

"I'll be right there."

Stan's tone indicated surprise. "It's 2 a.m. and he didn't even ask why you dragged him out of bed?"

"I imagine he'd do anything without question if it meant finding Emma."

"What will you do if he runs into cottage #3 and shoots both of them?"

"Is that before, or after, I help him shoot?"

"You take cheating on a spouse mighty serious, Sheriff."

"I know you don't think marriage vows are important so drop the subject. Let's determine our next move."

Twenty minutes later Lexie watched Devon run down the hill toward the cottage. She decided honesty was the only way to proceed. He'll play along or run back to his cheating wife."

His chest heaved as Lexie opened the door. Devon's words huffed, "What did you find out?"

"Sit down before you have a heart attack," Stan ordered.

"What about Emma?"

"Where is Cass tonight?" Lexie asked.

"She went shopping with a friend, an overnight trip. Did you bring me here to attack her? I'm not listening to this." He moved toward the door.

Stan stepped in front of Devon. "You need to listen. Sit down; it won't take long."

Devon pulled out a kitchen chair, "Tell me."

Stan leaned toward him, "Your wife is two doors down. We assume she's screwing your hired help, Kent."

Devon's previously pink face turned red. Sweat bubbles formed across his forehead. He looked like a man who just stuck his finger in a light socket.

Lexie pulled out a chair facing Devon. "Emma caught Cass and Kent embracing. Cass told Emma it meant nothing. She told Emma you'd be miserable if she told you. Kent and Cass had motive to get Emma out of the way. As long as Emma was around they risked her divulging their secret. Cass might lose you and your money—Kent his job."

"My money is important to Cass."

"When you came home from your business trip, the day Emma disappeared, was Cass at home?"

"No, the place was deserted."

"When did she get home?"

"She showed up around 9 p.m."

Stan butted in, "Why do you remember?"

"I was gone three days and my wife didn't quit shopping in time to have dinner with me. Do you think Cass and Kent hurt Emma?"

"There's no proof both, or either one, took her."

Stan chimed in, "But no proof they didn't either."

"They're in that cottage right now?"

"Yes," Lexie confirmed.

"Does one of you have a camera?"

A wicked grin crossed Stan's face. "Does it sound like a photo op? I'll get the camera from my place. I'm such a nice guy I'll even take the photos for you."

"While you're doing that I'll go home for a few minutes."

Sweat beads erupted on Lexie's chest.

"No photos until I get back, please. I don't want them to get spooked and take off." Devon disappeared out the front door.

Lexie stuttered, "You suppose he went after a gun?"

"I hope not. I want to go back to bed. Murders are a real timewaster, what with all the questions and evidence collection. Surely, he won't go that route."

"If he comes back with a loaded gun, perhaps you can convince him you don't want to be bothered with the aftermath."

"I'll stand guard by Kent's cottage until we figure out what he's up to," Stan volunteered.

"I'll stay here with my weapon handy."

The trip to Devon's condo was less than thirty minutes, but over an hour passed before his car pulled up in back of Lexie's cottage.

Lexie circled her rental, and caught sight of Tanner lugging an armful of ladies clothes away from their car.

"Devon, are you sure you want your son involved in this mess?"

"Positive, he'll drive my other car back home. Will you help carry Cass's stuff? We'll drop it in front of her sex nest."

Stan met them on the front lawn. "If you want photos, Devon, I'll take them first. They might hear us out front."

"Yes, they're very important."

Ten minutes later Stan returned. "I was able to take two shots through the window. After we get her stuff dumped I'll go in and give them a surprise."

After Cass's belongings were piled high in the front yard, Devon handed Tanner the key to her black Corvette. "Congratulations on your new ride, son. Take the car and go home."

"But, Dad, I want to see her face."

"Go home, son."

Tanner jogged to his new car.

"Time for those surprise photos, Stan."

"I'm on it."

Lexie and Devon waited outside #3.

A shriek from Cass, then a bellow from Kent, burst into the night air.

"Thanks for the memory," Stan yelled.

Lexie saw a vase fly toward Stan. He escaped, but glass pieces showered behind him.

"Stop him!" Cass screamed.

A naked Kent bellowed, "Bastard!" into the night.

Lexie pulled her gun and pointed it at Kent's genitals. "Let's talk, but first put on your clothes."

Devon and Stan followed Lexie into #3.

Cass pulled at Devon's arm. "I love you. Kent's nothing to me."

"Thanks, Bitch," Kent mumbled.

Devon pulled Cass's hand from his arm and dropped it without looking at her pleading face.

Lexie roughed her tone. "You two are my top suspects for Emma's disappearance."

Cass whimpered, "I'd never hurt Emma. She's like a daughter to me."

"Shut your mouth, Devon raged. Where were you the day she disappeared? You sure as hell weren't at home."

Kent's words shot out, "We were in New Orleans."

Devon finally looked at Cass. "You took him to our honeymoon hotel?"

"I know you'll forgive me, because you love me so much."

He pushed her away. "All you are is a mistake. If I find out you hurt Emma, you'll both have hell to pay."

Stan reached paper toward Kent. "Give me the name of that hotel. Both of you stick around town. If you take off, you'll look even more guilty."

"Arrest them!" Devon demanded.

Lexie's tone was apologetic, "We don't have enough evidence... yet."

"Phone me when you find out something." Devon slammed out the door.

Cass shrieked at Kent, "Look what you caused!"

"Me?"

"You've ruined my life," she wailed.

"You're the one who wanted in my jockeys."

"I'll go home," she stated. "Devon will forgive me."

Stan chuckled, "You aren't going anywhere, woman. Devon gave away your car."

She rushed out the front door, then collapsed on top of the pile of expensive clothes and shoes Devon left behind.

Lexie and Stan walked past.

"She's having a bad day," Stan joked.

"I think you're right for a change."

"Night," Lexie said as Stan stepped on the porch of #2.

"Same to you. I enjoyed our night out."

"Me too," Lexie called over her shoulder.

The bed in #1 was softer than ever. She fell asleep after the last thought of her day. *Maybe tomorrow one of them will admit where they left Emma's body.*

CHAPTER TWENTY-ONE

Tye's Case

Delia poured coffee for Tye, then herself. "Was that Jason on the phone?"

"He has another theory for me to check out."

Delia stirred creamer into her cup. "How's the case progressing?"

"There are some leads. Do the initials A.M. ring a bell?"

Delia blew into her coffee. "Not right offhand... hmm, A.M."

"I found the initials on a gold cross in Wendy's drawer. One of many crosses she hid."

"A collection of crosses? Strange."

"That's one of many weird things about Wendy. Betty claimed that dead people talked to Wendy. For all I know, A.M. may be one of the dead people."

Delia repeated, "Dead person with the initials A.M."

A bird chirped outside the window as the pair concentrated on the initials.

"Keep thinking about it," Tye requested. "Eventually, an answer may spring from one of our brains. I'll check death records at the courthouse later today."

Delia's words sang out, "Alan Moore."

"I don't recall that name."

"Alan died during your military service. A bullet ricocheted off a tree and hit him in the head when he was deer hunting."

"Who fired that bullet?"

"His father killed him. Moore's wife blamed him for Alan's death, but eventually forgave him. Alan's dad swore he wasn't drinking before the accident."

"Is the guy still around?"

"He lives less than ten miles out of town. Trey drives a bus for the school system."

Tye's flailing hand sent his coffee cup in motion. Sprinkles of coffee dotted the papers on his desk.

Delia scurried for a towel. Tye pushed papers to the side before the coffee seeped into them.

She blotted the desk.

"Thanks," Tye said. "I got excited."

"What about?"

"Trey Moore is one of the suspects in Wendy's death. Maybe Wendy knew Trey's negligence caused his son's death. If Wendy told him she knew the truth, he'd want to shut her up."

"This stuff is way out there." Delia limped back to her desk.

"Don't I know it. I'll hunt down Moore to hear what he has to say for himself."

"That sounds like an interesting conversation."

"For sure," Tye hurried out the door.

It didn't take long to reach his destination. Tye drove to the back of the high school, and pulled up to a metal bus barn. A couple of men lingered at the back door.

One man called to him, "Have you found that murderer?"

"I'm working on it." Tye walked toward them. "Have you guys heard any rumors?"

"Not a word," the short guy answered.

The other guy seconded, "Same here."

"Where can I find Trey Moore?"

"Inside."

"Thanks."

Gas, oil and emission smells combined to make the air inside the barn unpleasant.

Tye spoke loudly, "Trey Moore."

"In my office," he answered.

Tye walked toward the voice. A sign outside the office read *supervisor*.

Trey reached a hand across his desk. "What can I do for you, Deputy?"

After a brief handshake, Tye sat in a fold-up chair across from Trey. "I want to discuss Wendy's murder with you."

A dark cloud hovered in the small room. Trey croaked out one word, "Terrible." It looked like the big man was about to cry.

Moore's mouth clenched as his hands gripped the arms of the chair.

Tye fished the gold cross out of his pocket and dangled it in front of Trey's face. "Tell me about the cross. Did it belong to your son?"

"Yes."

"I found it in Wendy's things. Did she steal it?"

"I gave it to her."

"Why would you give away something that belonged to your dead child?"

Tears puddled under his eyes. "Wendy saved me, or maybe I should say God saved me through Wendy. She was the last kid on the bus five years ago when I stopped by her mailbox to let her out. I was eager for her to leave because I had big plans for the weekend...my suicide. I couldn't bear another day without my son."

"What about that day?" Tye's words sought to bring the man back.

"Wendy paused at the steps and turned toward me. She was tiny back then. Her brown hair was a mass of curls that surrounded her face. Eyes peaked out from beneath a lace of bangs across her forehead. The memory is so vivid."

Moore was caught in the memory. "Go on," Tye urged.

"Her hands clasped and held at her chest. She delivered my message in a whisper. Alan told me to tell you not to kill yourself. He said kids need your help. You must make a difference in their lives. His death wasn't your fault. You told him a hundred times to stay behind you when you shot. You'll see him in heaven. Your work on earth isn't finished. He can't be at peace until he knows you'll not harm yourself."

Tye watched as Trey fetched a white hankie from his pocket and mopped his tears.

"I sobbed like a two-hundred pound baby. That little sprite of a girl brought me a message from beyond. Her words changed my life. I started coaching sports, playing Santa, being a big brother and anything else that involved helping kids. I gave Wendy the gold cross because she saved my life."

Tye looked at the sincerity etched in the man's features and the truth in his tone. There was no doubt in his mind that Trey would never have harmed Wendy.

After a "thank you" to Moore, Tye walked to the high school. Gene, the janitor, seemed an unlikely killer, but he did clean up the building when the principal told him not to. Gene was the only person Tye hadn't questioned who seemed the least bit suspicious.

He stuck his head in Bradford's office. "I wanted you to know that I'm questioning Gene. Where is he?"

Bradford's welcoming smile dropped from his lips. "Gene is a kind man. He even carries out ladybugs that come inside. He was stung once because he tried to rescue a bee."

"I've got to follow the leads, Principal."

"Gene's in the basement. He has a chair and desk in the corner."

Tye found the young man sitting on the cement floor cleaning his tools. "Gene."

He jumped to attention when Tye spoke his name.

"Yes, Sir."

"Where should we sit to talk about Wendy's case?"

"I got a spot in the corner."

Tye followed him to an old wooden desk with a stained chair.

Gene pulled up a metal chair and motioned Tye to take the upholstered one behind the desk.

Tye's eyes surveyed the area. There weren't any personal items or photos on the desk. He looked up and his heart skipped a beat. An eighteen-inch, handmade, wooden cross hung on the wall behind the desk.

"I like the cross, Gene. Did you make it?"

"Yes."

"Do you make them for other people? It looks like a bigger version of the cross I found in Wendy's belongings. Did you make a cross for Wendy?"

His words stuttered out, "No... no, can't do that."

"Why not?"

"Principal told me to stay away from the girls. They're bad news."

"You're a healthy young fellow. There's nothing wrong with you liking girls. I heard Wendy had big boobs."

A red blush crept around his neck. "Don't talk ugly about Wendy."

"Why did you make the cross for her?"

"I didn't."

"Don't lie to me, Gene. Principal can fire you, but I can throw you in jail for a long time. Why did you give Wendy the cross?"

"That Star girl..."

"Starla?"

"Starla got in the hall closet with me and started screaming like crazy. She said I touched her nasty place. When I ran out, Wendy was standing outside the door."

Gene paused, his words halted by emotion.

"Go on, son."

Starla ran to the principal's office. He came and got me. She sat there screaming that I hurt her. I didn't hurt anybody. I scrub the cafeteria floors after lunch everyday and her fit made me late."

"Principal Bradford told me that you're a hard worker."

"Starla's mother showed up. She yelled, too. She said Bradford better fire me or she'd raise hell until he lost his job."

"What does Wendy have to do with this?"

"Wendy came in Principal's door. She didn't even knock. She pointed at Star girl and said, 'She's lying, Mr. Bradford. I heard everything she said to Gene. She tricked Gene to get him in the closet. She told him the girl's restroom was out of paper towels. Soon as the door closed, she started screaming.'"

"I assume Mr. Bradford believed Wendy?"

"He did after Star stopped screaming and started using bad words. Star said Wendy had hell to pay for messing with her."

"What did Starla's mother say?"

"She told me 'sorry'. Principal told her to keep Star home for three days."

"She was suspended?"

"That was the word, I think. After a little bit Principal thanked Wendy and sent her to class."

"What did he say to you?"

"He told me to stay away from the girls, 'cause they're bad news.' I must look down, if one talks to me."

"You made Wendy the cross?"

"I wanted to thank her. Wendy said to make her a cross from wood, or draw one on paper. She liked crosses better than anything."

"I know your cross was special to her because I found it wrapped in a red scarf."

Gene's words stumbled out, "Don't tell Principal I gave Wendy a cross."

"No reason for me to tell. I'm sorry I took so much of your work time. Have a good day."

Tye took two stair steps at a time. No killer was found, but a question was answered. Now he knew why Starla pushed Wendy's head in the toilet.

CHAPTER TWENTY-TWO

Lexie's Case

Lexie opened the door to let in the fresh morning air. There sat Stan, on the step, with a restaurant bag in hand.

"Food for me?"

"Bad news and breakfast," Stan replied.

Lexie sat on the step beside him. "I don't want to know."

"Nor did I want to hear that their story panned out. The cheaters were in New Orleans until after Emma's disappearance. The cops in New Orleans checked and rechecked for me. The hotel manager even remembered Cass, because she was a demanding bitch."

"I feel like spilling out a stream of cuss words. I've never had a case that ended so dismally."

"I've had a couple and it's hard to take. Eat this egg-bacon biscuit to give yourself something to chew on, besides your ego."

"What time are we leaving for the airport?"

"Within the hour; I'll pack right now."

Lexie looked toward cottage #3. "I see Cass hasn't cleaned up her clothes pile. I bet she isn't used to picking up after herself. I'll stay inside to avoid any contact with the pair."

"I'll knock on your door when I'm ready to leave."

Lexie finished her breakfast at the table. She put on white shorts and a blue sleeveless shirt. She pulled out each drawer and tossed belongings to the bed. Soon the clothes were folded and bathroom items packed away. As soon as the town meeting ended, she was homeward bound.

A knock on the door and she and Stan left for the airport.

Lexie stopped at the only traffic light in town. "Are you staying at your job?"

"I check in tomorrow morning. I'm not sure where getting fired, then brought back to work leaves me. They may not give me a choice."

"What will you do if you get to choose?"

" I'll stay until I find another job. I require food and a roof over my head."

"You're good at the job. You were patient and kind with Kylie."

"Is that surprise in your voice?"

"Probably, I've never known you to show any respect for women." Lexie didn't manage to keep the sarcasm out of her tone.

"They're children. A whole different female population."

"True."

"What's next for you, Sheriff Lexie?"

"I'm already packed. I'll attend the town meeting, out of curiosity, then head home. Sarah can come back and finish her investigation. I have nothing left to give."

"Turn right at the next light then you can pull in front of the airport. It was an adventure," Stan gave her braid a tug.

"You speak the truth."

"Can we be friends if I change from a male chauvinist asshole pig? I think that's all the names you've called me."

"You mean we'll go shopping together and buy purses?"

"Bar fights and football games are my preferences."

"You want me to be your guy friend?"

He gave her a smooch on the cheek. "Kissing cousins would be better."

Lexie smiled, "We'll give it a long distance try."

"Later," he snatched his bag from the back seat.

The flurry of happiness she felt lasted about sixty seconds. Immediately, her head and heart returned to Emma's case.

After forty minutes of driving, she reached the turn to Devon's condo.

The front door opened as she walked up the sidewalk. Devon's words rushed out, "Did they take Emma?"

"Stan did the follow-up. Cass and Kent were both out of state."

"Come and sit," he invited.

"I only have ten minutes. I suppose you're going to the town meeting?"

"Swinson said he had an important announcement and wanted Tanner and me to attend. Does he know what happened to Emma?"

Lexie's head shook. "I have no idea. I'll find out when you do. I'm sure this is none of my business, but you don't seem r upset about losing Cass."

"I knew she wasn't right for me, but I felt lost without my wife. I tried to replace her with the first person who came along. I learned quickly it's not easy to replace the love of your life."

Lexie's gaze dropped to the floor, "A lesson I sometimes forget."

"I won't ever forget it again."

"I better head out. See you at the meeting."

"Yes," Devon answered.

·····•••●•●•••····

Men, women and children, from two months to ninety-two years, crowded the town hall. No chairs left, Lexie squeezed between two men near the back of the room.

Chief Swinson stood at a podium. His sleeves were rolled up, a cup of coffee in his hand and eyes bloodshot. He greeted first one person then another by name.

Lexie visually scanned the room but didn't see Danny.

"Gentlemen," Swinson's voice burst out to quiet the crowd.

"A short but positive message for each of my fellow citizens. We've all worried about the safety of our daughters, and the economic upheaval to our community as the result of the disappearance of Emma Chandler. I'm proud to tell you those worries are past. No need for vacationers to leave town.

No need to worry about the safety of your children. Emma's captor is in jail where he belongs and will stay until he goes to trial. There'll be no mercy for Zane Sullivan. He'll face the full punishment for men who prey on teenagers."

Virgil's voice pierced from the back of the room. "My grandson didn't take that girl. He's a good boy."

Swinson's voice, strong and confident, filled the room. "Your grandson's DNA was on Emma's backpack. He was the last one with her, admitted they argued, and lied about dropping her off at the theater. A dumped guy who couldn't handle the rejection. Best keep your mouth shut, Virgil. For all I know, you're an accessory. You're always spouting about running off the summer people. Looks like Zane helped with your cause."

Lexie heard Virgil's running steps down the center aisle. People in back parted to let him through. She'd not connected that Virgil and Zane were relatives.

Someone yelled, "You better get out old man, before we string you up with your grandson."

Swinson didn't address the heckler, instead his words boomed into the microphone. "Friends, go about your business with peace of mind."

People shuffled toward the back door.

A pain stabbed at Lexie's temple. *Swinson found a scapegoat to calm the masses. It's more than an innocent boy jailed, more than people with a false confidence of safety. It's about an abductor no one searches for who can snatch another girl at any moment.*

CHAPTER TWENTY-THREE

Tye's Case

Tye lumbered back to his truck. The long shifts and the dead ends in the case wore him out. He hoped to have Wendy's case solved before Lexie returned, but he didn't catch a break. Now Trey was off the suspect list, too.

Back at the office, he unrolled the newspaper. The desire to read left him as his brain resumed the search for answers. His words spit into the air, "Who killed you, Wendy?"

Delia pushed through the door with a bag from Dixie's. She swung her big purse to the floor. "I brought you an early lunch."

"I missed breakfast."

"Jamie told me you're not eating or sleeping much. She's worried about you."

"Good to know that she still cares."

"Of course, she does." Delia handed him the bag.

The smells of a burger and fries forced Tye to the realization that his body felt way low on fuel. Two French fries later his cell phone rang.

"It's Jason."

"I wasn't expecting to hear from you until after school. Is anyone listening?"

"I'm curious to find out if you arrested Trey."

"I talked to him. He's innocent."

Jason's voice trembled. "But...it had to be him. I was sure."

"I thought so, too, but don't worry. I'll keep looking until the killer is brought to justice. He'll pay."

"They're holding a memorial assembly this afternoon for Wendy."

"How do you feel about that, Jason?"

"All of them are hypocrites. They'll act all sad and cry like they cared."

"What would Wendy think?"

"She'd forgive them, but I won't. I told Wendy they all had to pay, but she wouldn't listen. Now she's dead." His next words rushed out. "There's the bell. I've got to hurry to the auditorium. The principal asked me to say a few words about Wendy."

"Okay. I'll talk to you tomorrow."

Tye looked down at the newspaper. A point of light reflected from the window. It hit a headline on the right side of the paper:

SCHOOL SHOOTING—THREE DEAD

Tye's heart leapt. *What did Jason say? 'They all had to pay... an assembly for Wendy.'* Now a streak of light pointed to a school shooting. Tye's heartbeat increased: Jason's erratic tone, hurried words, and hatred over the phone. *Was Wendy sending a message? Not logical, but possible?*

Tye barked orders at Delia. "Call the Highway Patrol. Tell them to send three units to the high school for backup."

He ran toward the door. Delia's words followed, "What for?"

He heard her, but didn't answer. For all he knew it was for nothing, but he couldn't risk the kids getting shot. A shooting in a high school auditorium would result in a devastating number of deaths and injuries.

The cruiser hit 85 mph on the straight ways then dropped to 80 as he maneuvered the curves. Once there, he slammed on the brakes and ran up the cement steps.

He halted at the double doors to the auditorium. Fearful that Jason might see him and panic, Tye mixed in with a group of students entering the assembly. Then he moved to the right side where teachers stood.

A girl led a prayer. Jason sat on a chair near the podium. His right hand stuck in a suit pocket.

A teacher vacated the seat beside Jason and came forward. "Jason Durring has a few words about Wendy, his best friend."

A few giggles trickled in the air as Jason wobbled forward.

His words screeched out, "You're all evil and deserve to die! Your cruel words killed my friend, and now I'll kill you!"

Tye walked toward him. "Jason, don't do this. Wendy didn't want people hurt."

"They deserve to die," he raged.

"This will ruin your life."

"They already destroyed it." He raised the gun, "Goodbye devils."

Tye's shot resounded in the room and made a gut-wrenching racket as it hit the firearm in Jason's hand. The impact threw Jason to the floor, and his gun flew to the back of the stage.

Cries and gasps were heard all around as Tye maneuvered through the hoard of terrified kids.

He bent over Jason.

Jason's eyes shot daggers. "You saved the demons."

Tye pulled him up and escorted him through the throng of frightened students.

Principal Bradford stood ashen-faced at the auditorium door. "If you hadn't showed up, kids would have died. How did you know?"

"A miracle—a message. I don't really know."

Four highway patrolmen walked toward him as he handcuffed Jason.

"What's going on?" one trooper questioned.

"Jason's plan for a school shooting didn't work out."

"That secretary of yours didn't give us information. I didn't know what we were getting into."

"I didn't tell Delia anything. Went on my gut. It could've been a total debacle."

"What's our role?"

"I shot the gun out of his hand in the auditorium. Your investigation will ensure the accuracy of my story. Call if you have questions. I'm driving Jason to the hospital to get his hand checked."

In the passenger seat Jason sat wordless as he held his injured right hand in the left.

Tye's brain worked to understand Jason's actions. Perhaps Jason wanted to kill them all in hopes he'd luck out and actually get Wendy's murderer. Perhaps the news Trey wasn't arrested blasted his last hope. Then again maybe telling him to sneak around for information put him in the position of feeling responsible for finding the killer.

Tye wanted to hear Jason's reasoning for the school shooting. Maybe something in his answer would support his case. "Why did you do it, Jason?"

"I trusted Wendy and wanted her safe. I told her I was going to shoot the demons during the Awards Assembly. I asked her to play sick and go to the nurse's office."

Tye's breath drew in, *Jason killed Wendy.* He forced calmness into his tone. "Wendy knew you planned to kill the students?"

"Yes. She threatened to rat on me, tell Bradford."

"Is that the day she died?"

"She planned to ruin everything. I was killing them for both of us. She tried to talk me out of it, but I wouldn't let the devils off free."

"You murdered her so she couldn't stop you from killing them?"

"My only friend was tattling to save the demons. She told you, didn't she? Even dead, she sold me out."

Tye paused, then a memory rose in his head. "I asked her earlier today who killed her. A little later the phone rang and you said, 'It's Jason'."

"Where are you taking me?"

"We're going to the hospital to get your hand checked. Your parents are meeting us there."

"Did they sound mad on the phone?"

"Heartbroken," was Tye's only response.

"Where will I go after the hospital?"

"I'll take you to the courthouse to go before a judge to admit your guilt. You'll probably stay in the county jail a few days. It's difficult to find a bed in a juvenile facility."

Silence consumed the rest of the drive to the emergency room. One thought stuck in Tye's head. *I found the killer by accident—or did Wendy help me?*

CHAPTER TWENTY-FOUR

Lexie's Case

Lexie drove to the cottage to grab her bag and pay the bill. Virgil sat on the front step. He stood as she walked toward him.

"Zane didn't hurt that girl. He's a good boy—too kind at times. Loans his buddies money, helps me out and never asks for anything in return. Swinson ambushed Zane to get everybody off his drunken back."

Lexie studied his face as she spoke. "As far as I know, what Swinson said is true. Zane fought with Emma, last one with her, and lied about dropping her off in town. The DNA confirmed his presence with her."

"He carried that backpack to the beach. Zane told me it was heavy because it held their drinks and suntan lotion."

"Logical, Virgil, but it still looks bad. A good attorney can get him off if he's innocent."

"You met him, talked to him. Do you think he's guilty?"

"My opinion is based on my heart, not the facts. If this happened in my town, I would arrest him."

"What did your heart feel?"

"I believed Zane, but that's irrelevant. I have no proof, and every possible suspect I've come across has evaporated upon close inspection. As I said, find a good attorney—not from around here."

"You're the only one who thinks he's innocent."

"Virgil, I have to get home to my baby and job."

Lexie pulled a pen and paper out of her purse. "Here's Sarah Chandler's phone number. She's the one you need to talk to. She'll fight to make sure the right person pays for the crime."

Virgil walked toward the shoreline. Lexie entered her small sanctuary and sank into the mattress.

Four hours later, she awoke. The late afternoon sun peeked through the window shades. Her mostly sleepless night had caught up with her. Now she had no desire to head out on unfamiliar highways in the dark. She resolved to start early in the morning.

A message from Tye lit up her phone.

"What's up, Bro?"

"You sound groggy."

"I fell asleep, I won't head out until the morning. Any news?"

"I arrested Wendy's killer."

"Don't leave me in suspense. Who killed her?"

"Jason Durring admitted killing her. He thought I figured it out—I hadn't. I should've realized that he found another person for me to investigate every time I ruled someone out."

"He killed his best friend?"

"Hatred for his classmates far outweighed his love for Wendy. He killed her because she threatened to report his school shooting plan to the principal."

"Were students hurt?"

"I stopped him before he fired."

"You're a hero."

"Wendy's the hero."

"Are you saying Wendy told you?"

"I don't know. It appeared she sent a message, but maybe only a coincidence. A beam of light hit my open newspaper and happened to illuminate a school shooting out of state."

"Wow."

"Do you have any leads on Emma's case?"

"Swinson arrested Emma's boyfriend."

"I hear doubt in your voice."

"I don't think he did it, but Sarah will have to sort it out."

"Sorry you didn't receive a message from the dead."

"I needed divine intervention. I still don't have a clue as to what happened to Emma."

"I know that'll eat on you, Sis. But, as you said earlier, it's Sarah's problem."

"Congratulations, I'm glad your case is solved."

"Thanks. See you soon."

Lexie pulled a sweatshirt from her bag. She straightened the hood as she confronted the outside mist. The restaurant offered hot food and people noise. She'll kill a few hours before returning to bed.

Lexie got quietness instead of conversation. The waitress informed her that storm warnings were out, which caused everyone to vacate the beach. Lexie put a coin in the machine and played a Blake Shelton song. The chicken and dumplings tasted like gourmet food, or maybe hunger skewed her opinion. The last bite finished, she wandered to the ocean's edge.

The turbulence inside her was reflected in the waves. They were calm her first few days here, but now the surges were powerful. She remembered that Amos mentioned the angry ocean, and it appears she'll experience it firsthand tonight. *Too bad I didn't head home as intended.*

Emma vanished and there were no leads left to follow and no hope. She didn't take failure well. It ate at her chest and put her brain in turmoil. *What did I miss?*

"Lexie." The word sounded from behind her, almost lost in the ocean's roar.

She acknowledged the waving hand in the distance.

Deputy Danny moved toward her. "I wasn't sure when you were heading back to Oklahoma. Came to say goodbye. My sister's wedding is day after tomorrow so I'm off for a few days. Thanks for all your work on Emma's case."

"I'm leaving first thing in the morning. There's no reason to thank me when the case is left unsolved."

"Chief thinks Zane did it."

"Do you?"

"No, but I'm prejudice. Zane and I were friends in junior high. Chief Ted is right. The evidence points to Zane, whether I like it or not."

"Diffee is short a deputy. Would you consider moving to Oklahoma?"

"Thanks for the offer, but I can't desert Ted."

Lexie grumbled, "He needs to desert his bottle and stop leaving you all the work."

"He'll get better over time. A great officer until his daughter died."

"When was that?"

"It'll be four months tomorrow."

"Did she die of natural causes?"

"Her drowning almost destroyed him. He and his daughter argued, she threatened suicide then stormed out. He didn't follow her. Her body washed up on shore January 31st. I think he'll get better over time. I plan to stay here until he does."

"I've enjoyed working with you. Phone if you change your mind about the job."

"Will do," Danny offered a firm handshake, then climbed back up the hill.

Lexie returned her rear to the rock wall. Her brain searched for an answer. What was it? What did I miss? A coincidence? A pattern?

CHAPTER TWENTY-FIVE

Lexie's Case

The waves came in faster. Dark clouds dimmed the sun's last rays. The depth of its danger compromised the beauty of the ocean.

A spark ignited in Lexie's head—a chain formed. Amos' daughter committed suicide on New Year's Eve, December 31st. The Swinson girl's body was found January 31st. Misty Rose disappeared the last week of March. Now it was the last week in May, the thirty-first tomorrow. Does this mean something? Four girls lost the last week of the month around the thirty-first. When did it begin? Her brain concentrated on the lists of girls she'd seen. Eight girls were found in the sex trafficking bust, and a couple of others designated as runaways. None of them fit the disappearance pattern.

She jumped to her feet. There was another girl: Amos' oldest daughter. She died last year—on Halloween—October 31st. What did Amos say my first day here? He called the ocean a raging beast that ate humans.

Lexie ran to the cottage and jerked the black hooded rain jacket out of her packed bag Underwear and make-up spilled to the floor. She pocketed her gun and jogged toward the Jeep.

Danny was headed to a wedding, so she left a phone message for Swinson. Aware he might never listen to her words.

The curvy road to Amos' house coincided with her twisted thoughts. What's my theory? It's not likely Amos is feeding teenagers to the ocean.

Lexie parked her Jeep yards from Amos' house. She noted lights from three windows. A couple of lanterns hung over the boat dock.

The rock and sand terrain made it difficult to stay camouflaged. Soon darkness will give her better cover. There was no sign of Amos on board the houseboat.

She crouched below the first lit window then moved slowly upward to peek in. No one sat in the living room. She moved to the next rectangle of light. A small slit between the curtain panels gave her visual access to the room. Four people sat eating at the kitchen table: Amos, Natalia, likely his wife and his mother. Still freaked from her sex trafficking experience, Lexie ducked down, fearful that someone might catch a glimpse of her. Lexie ran toward the boat without cover.

The old houseboat rocked as she climbed aboard. Sprinkles of rain gained momentum as she surveyed the beer cans and food wrappers. She knelt to search a canvas bag, unsure of what she looked for. A wave assaulted the boat sending it into a turbulent rock. Lexie's hands pressed her belly in an attempt to calm the chicken and dumplings. The ocean roared around her.

She startled as the butt of a rifle poked into her back. She turned slowly.

A lantern glare hit his furrowed face. "What are you doing here, woman?"

"I was looking for you. I saw the lanterns and thought you were out battening down the hatches before the storm hit."

Amos lowered his gun. "What do you want?"

"I'm still looking for information on Emma's case."

"I told you already that I don't know nothin' about that."

Lexie bent forward, "I feel sick. Where's the toilet?"

Amos pointed toward the steps.

She hurried down and bent over the stool. Vomit rushed out. A couple of minutes later she glanced back. Amos no longer stared from the steps. She pulled shut the door to the head. Her body stooped over the toilet, while her eyes searched the small space. Searching for—she didn't know what. Her eyes caught on a crack at the base of the sink cabinet—a striped barrette barely peeked out. Lexie thought of Emma's room—all things zebra.

Now she was positive Emma was in this boat. It appeared she'd left another clue for her Aunt Sarah.

Still no sound from Amos; *my retching grossed him out.* Lexie moved into the space outside the head, hoping that Amos would think she was still puking. She required more proof. He can claim Emma left the barrette when she visited his daughter.

She wanted clothes or blood splatter. *Where would he hide the evidence?*

Fishing gear was strung across a long wood box that served as a bench down one side of the boat. Lexie attempted to pull up the top, but nails held it closed. A rustle from above sent a chill down her spine. She flattened against the wall. Seconds later she heard footsteps moving away. A hammer lay near the bench. Lexie stuck the claw under the corner, then waited for the next wave to hit. While the outside noise filled the boat, she heaved the claw with all her might. The bench top creaked open a couple of inches. Lexie stuck her fingers in the space and pulled up.

A gasp burst out—Emma's body. Her mouth was held shut by a dirty red bandanna. Her arms and legs were tied with rope. Emma's bugged eyes blinked. *She's alive!*

"It's okay," Lexie whispered. "I'm a friend of your Aunt Sarah." She quickly untied Emma's arms. She purposely left the gag in place fearful the girl would yell out in terror. "I hear him coming. Here's my gun. If he's the one who opens the bench, shoot him."

A voice yelled from the top deck and steps sounded. "Get out of here, Sheriff. You can puke outside."

Lexie lowered the bench lid and sat on its surface.

He stood in front of her. "You've messed with my bench." The butt of his rifle poked into her temple. "Too bad you must die tonight."

"Why did you kill those girls, Amos?"

"I sacrificed them to Poseidon. He's the god of water and the sea. I gave him girls so he wouldn't take my Natalia. She's the only daughter I have left. Poseidon took Hannah and Crystal."

"There's no ocean god, Amos. The deaths of your daughters were an accident and a suicide. Their deaths had nothing to do with Poseidon wanting sacrifices. Your sorrow screwed up your logic. Please don't kill another child."

His windblown hair stuck in greasy spikes. His gaze wandered, but never reached Lexie's face. The mad man waved his rifle and shouted, "I must sacrifice Emma to save my daughter, and now you must die, too!"

The rope burned Lexie's wrist as he pulled it tight, then maneuvered the ends around the stairrail to anchor her in place. She heard the start-up racket from the engine, and felt the boat pull away from shore.

She squirmed and wiggled. The rope bit against her skin as she fought its confines. Finally, one hand slid out and released the other one, then she unknotted the rope from the rail.

"Don't shoot, Emma." Lifting the bench, Lexie put a finger to her lips, retrieved the gun, and then unknotted the gag.

Emma's mouth moved silently as if working out the soreness. Lexie untied her feet.

"Take me to Daddy," she begged.

"Amos plans to kill us. But he has a rude awakening coming."

"Please take me home."

"Be brave a little longer, Emma. We've got to work together."

The girl's body trembled. "I can't take anymore."

"I'll help you out of the box. Your body is stiff from being locked up, so move slowly."

"No," Emma whimpered.

"Yes, you can and will," Lexie hissed. "Now move."

The girl pulled to sitting then situated her hands on the edge of the bench to boost herself to standing with Lexie's support. Reaching one leg over, she fell sideways. Lexie eased her to the floor."

"My legs are sore."

"You were inert too long."

"I can't walk," she moaned.

"Force yourself to move. You left clues so I know you're smart enough to understand that you can't sit around and wait for Amos to kill us."

"My body hurts."

"We're getting you to the toilet. Either stand-up or crawl."

Emma reached up and Lexie hoisted her and moved toward the head.

"Sit on the seat. Move your legs and arms constantly to get some motion back. I'll shut the door."

Oily hair puffed around Emma's face, but lay flat at the back of her head. A forehead vein throbbed. "No! No! Don't leave me. He'll kill you, then me." She clasped Lexie's arm.

Lexie handed Emma the gun. "Take this. If Amos gets the best of me you'll have to kill him to save yourself. Don't hesitate if he opens the door. Shoot him. Have you fired a gun before?"

"Daddy taught me how to shoot."

"I'll yell 'all safe' when I get Amos secured."

Emma pointed the gun straight at the opening as Lexie shut the door.

Lexie grabbed the hammer and made her way to the top of the steps. The waves tossed from side to side and her stomach protested. *No way belly, you've got to hold it in. There's no time for vomiting.*

She slipped off the steps toward the stern.

The boat slowed at the rocky shore. She watched as Amos tethered the boat to a rickety ramp, then jumped back onto the boat. His cap blew toward her hiding place.

"Shit," he yelped as he leaped to save his hat.

As he leaned forward, Lexie swung the hammer to the side of his head.

Shock and pain roared out, "Devil woman!"

His hands grabbed her neck. Lexie kicked at his legs and pressed her arms between his to disengage the grasp on her throat. He grabbed her hair and pulled her to the side of the boat. Her legs kicked aimlessly as her hand clawed toward his face. At the edge of the boat, he shoved her off the side. She fought to keep her head above water. Amos jabbed at the water with a long hook. She grabbed and jerked with all her might. He stumbled over the side. Lexie swam beneath him and pulled at his flailing legs.

She surfaced for air, then dove back down to pull him under again. His struggle diminished with each second, then stopped. Her chest on fire, she swam to the surface. She waited too long. She touched the side of the boat, but didn't have the strength to pull up.

A hand reached out. Swinson leaned over, "Hold on, Lexie." He grasped her hand and pulled her onto the boat.

She gasped and coughed water. Points of blood erupted on her legs and arms from the fight.

"Where's Amos?"

Lexie pointed toward the water.

Swinson's eyes surveyed the ocean surface, then he knelt beside Lexie. "No sign of him."

She forced out words, "Emma's in the head. She has my gun."

Swinson stood.

"Wait," Lexie yelped, "tell her who you are and yell 'all safe.' I'm afraid she'll shoot through the door."

Lexie sat up and leaned forward. Thank God, no gun shot.

Swinson carried Emma and laid her beside Lexie, then he untethered the vessel and headed back to shore, leaving his small boat behind. Lexie noted the slowness of the vessel and Swinson's visual search of the water.

I purposely drowned Amos. Perhaps better not to admit, since I'd have to stay longer. We fought in the water, Amos died and Swinson saved me; a simple story of two people giving out in the water.

"Your dad is heartbroken, Emma. He was terrified that you were gone forever.."

"I didn't think I'd see anyone again. Why are you here?"

"I'm a friend of your Aunt Sarah. I'm a sheriff in Oklahoma."

"Did you find my clues?"

"You're very clever. That's how we knew you didn't drown, and how I knew you were on Amos' boat. Do you have any pain?"

"I'm hungry, thirsty and sore." Soft sobs heaved her chest.

Lexie wrapped her arms around the girl. "You're safe now."

Ted spoke into his radio. "Chief Swinson here. I'm transporting a couple of females. We'll show up at the hospital in about an hour."

"I'm fine," Lexie said.

Swinson ignored her protest.

Once the three were in the patrol car, Swinson made a call. "Devon, it's Chief Swinson. You and Tanner meet us at the emergency room. Emma is okay, but will need examined before you take her home."

Lexie heard Devon's words cry out, "Emma is alive!"

"That lady sheriff found her. We'll tell you the story later. Head to the hospital."

When they pulled up to the emergency room entrance, Devon and Tanner rushed toward them followed by a couple of newspaper reporters.

Devon pulled Emma into his arms. "I love you so much my precious girl."

"I love you, too, Daddy."

Tanner looked at Lexie. "You're soaked."

"I almost drowned. Chief Swinson saved me."

"Who had Emma?" a reporter called out.

Swinson answered, "Amos Hicks."

"Why did he take her?"

Swinson pointed to Lexie, "Tell the reporters your theory."

"Amos' oldest two daughters died in the ocean on the thirty-first days of October and December. He sacrificed teen girls on the thirty-first day of the following months for fear the ocean would consume his only living child."

"What is the significance of the thirty-first?" the reporter asked.

"His oldest daughter died on Halloween. It's the day of the dead. His second daughter left a suicide note that said the ocean beckoned her. I assume Amos's grief-tortured brain decided that the thirty-first was when the ocean required a sacrifice. He became so obsessed with keeping his third daughter safe that he murdered girls, and sacrificed them to Poseidon."

"Our chief was a hero?"

"He saved my life when he pulled me out of the water."

"Sheriff Lexie is the hero. She found Emma, so put the praise where it belongs or I'll throw you in jail."

The reporters laughed.

Swinson motioned, "Let's head back to your vehicle. I'll drop you off, then tell Amos' family the man is a murderer and dead to boot."

Lexie shivered in the front seat. Swinson turned on the heater and pointed the slats toward Lexie.

"Thanks," she said. "This may sound rude, but I'm curious."

"Speak your mind."

"Why weren't you drunk tonight?"

"Today is the four month anniversary of Gretchen's death—my daughter. I always spend the day with her at the cemetery. It's my fault she's dead. She ran out of the house after we had an argument, and I didn't go after her. She threatened to hurt herself, but I thought she was manipulating me to get her way. She drowned because of me."

"Chief, I think Amos murdered your daughter."

"What?"

His daughters died on October 31st and December 31st. Gretchen's body was found on January 31st. A teenager named Misty Rose disappeared the last week of March. Emma was to die on May 31st. I believe that your daughter was one of Amos' human sacrifices."

"He murdered Gretchen?"

"She fits the pattern. Do you have other children?"

"I have three sons."

"Stay sober for them."

Swinson said his words softly as if talking to himself. "Gretchen didn't die because of me."

Lexie directed him to the Jeep location.

"You okay to go it alone?" he asked.

"I'm fine."

"Drop by my office before you head out of town tomorrow. Got to write up your statement."

"I'll be there first thing in the morning."

Lexie slid into the seat, then quickly turned on the heat. It crossed her mind that she might never feel warm again. The only things she wanted at this point were dry clothes and a soft bed. She was so tired by the time she reached the cottage, that she was unsure of the ability to drag herself to the front door.

She shed her clothes and stepped into a hot shower. The warmest nightclothes she found weren't warm at all—a tee and pink boxers. The pillow felt so fluffy she buried her head in its softness. Soon her body closed down for the rest of the short night.

CHAPTER TWENTY-SIX

Lexie's Case

Lexie woke at 6 a.m. on alert as to why she woke so suddenly after a mere three hours of sleep. She listened, but heard only chirping birds and the light hum of ocean waves. There it was again—a sound from the porch. She pulled on jeans and a red T-shirt, then looked out the front window. Virgil and Zane waited on the porch.

"What are you men up to?"

They turned at her voice.

"Swinson said you were leaving today. We wanted to say thank you before you took off."

"You're very welcome. A lucky fluke that I figured it out at the last minute."

"I don't believe in flukes," Virgil said. "We are guided from beyond."

Remembering Wendy's case, Lexie nodded.

Zane held her right hand in both of his. "I could've spent the rest of my life in prison. Thank you for saving me."

"You're a fine young man and I'm glad I helped you."

Virgil lifted a hand, "We'll head on out. Have a safe trip."

Zane called as he looked back, "Thanks again."

Lexie went in, sat on a kitchen chair and considered brewing coffee, but decided it required too much effort. The buzz of her cell phone sent her running toward her purse. She sank into the armchair to answer.

"Hello, Sarah."

"I can't thank you enough for finding Emma. You've got to admit, however, that I was right about my family not being involved."

The jab activated Lexie's temper.

Sarah continued, "I don't think there's any way I can ever repay you."

"No payment is required. I don't want help from a detective who declares people innocent because their relatives. Have a good life. Goodbye." Lexie pushed the off button. *That felt good!*

···•••●●•••···

Lexie arrived at the Chief's office at 7 a.m. Swinson commenced the interrogation at 7:03.

"A simple story," Lexie began. "Amos pushed me into the water then tried to hold me under with a long poled hook. I caught hold of it and pulled him in. We fought, he drowned, and I almost did. Even if I wanted to save him, I didn't have enough strength to do so." Lexie looked toward Swinson. "You know that's true, since you had to save me."

"Of course, I know."

Devon, Tanner and Emma entered the office.

Devon spoke, "There's not enough thanks in the world to express what you did for my family. There should be words beyond 'thank you,' but I cannot find them."

"I'm glad you have your girl back."

Emma wrapped her arms around Lexie. "Thank you a million."

"No, thanks a zillion," Tanner corrected. "My sister was never good at math."

"Glad she has you to assist her," Lexie joked.

"No kidding," Tanner laughed.

Emma squeezed his shoulder and stuck out her tongue.

Lexie turned her attention back to Swinson. "If you're finished with me, I'd like to go home."

"We'll hunt you down in Oklahoma if we have more questions," Swinson said.

"I'm not too hard to find."

Swinson's voice followed her to the door. "I have a million thanks for you, too."

Lexie gave the group a final wave.

Driving out of town she took the scenic highway with the ocean view. Someday she planned to visit the ocean again, preferably when a mentally ill man wasn't drowning girls. On highway 59 she caught site of her blinking message light. Unfortunately, she pushed the button.

"I think your mom should be the one to tell you that guy Red, you thought was so wonderful, eloped to Eureka Springs with Gina. It didn't take him long to move on. Call me when you get home."

The calm in the weather coincided with the stillness in Lexie's heart. *Perhaps it's better to know that a love is lost instead of waiting for a miracle.*

She answered her cell phone as the first note played.

"Are you okay, Sis? Mom told me she sprang the news about Red."

"She did it in her usual abrasive fashion. But yes, I'm okay. It's probably better to know that the door is closed."

"Are you headed home?"

"On my way."

"Red left Sky with Jamie."

"Good."

"One more piece of news. The Mayor picked your opponent for the November election."

"Who?"

"The man we think, but can't prove, is the county drug kingpin."

"It'll be an interesting campaign. I'll see you at work tomorrow afternoon."

Lexie turned off the phone and pushed the radio button. Something needed to fill her head other than thoughts of Red. As soon as the words from the song hit her ears she clicked off the radio. She dug in her purse, but was unable to find a tissue. Tears made paths down her cheeks and dropped from her chin.

Lexie said aloud, "I will always love you Red Anderson, but you've moved on and I'll do the same."

Acknowledgements

Thank you to the following individuals who provided encouragement, specialized information and/or recommendations during the writing process: Officer Steven Roberts, Kayla Grimes (teen consultant), Bill Wetterman, Myrna Kurle, Karen Cornell, Mark H. Jones, Lawrence Welch, Marcus Jones, and Dan Case.

Cover Art: Tara Mayberry, www.teaberrycreative.com

Ryan Cantrell's book *Modern Slavery: Investigating Human Trafficking* was a reference book for *Murder and Beyond.*

Author's website: www.donnawelchjones.com

More Sheriff Lexie Wolfe Novels

Killing the Secret - Book 1
Who is murdering the women who played on a championship high school basketball team twenty years ago? Sheriff Lexie Wolfe searches for the sin that put them on the kill list.

Deadly Search - Book 2
Sheriff Lexie Wolfe is entangled in a web of deceit as she searches for her father's murderer. Her mother may be the reason Lexie's father was killed. If she finds her father's killer what price will she pay for revenge?

Terror's Grip - Book 3
Lexie's right arm suspends above her, held by a chain attached to a two-inch metal clamp around her wrist. The chain trails through a broken cellar window. Her left hand fists and punches forward as if a boxing bag, or her captor's new face, dangles in front of her. Lexie's scream fills the cold darkness. "I WON'T DIE WEAK!"

Deranged Justice-Book 5
Local citizens panic when Sheriff Lexie doesn't solve a series of bizarre murder cases. She is removed from office pending an investigation of incompetence and criminal activity. An irrationally jealous woman and a man who demands custody of Lexie's adopted nephew add more turmoil to her life.

Her Dying Message-Book 6
Sheriff Lexie's tears blur the body that lies face down on the rocks. Her scream catches in the wind and carries to the treetops. A family member was shot at close range-murdered. Her pursuit of evidence is hampered by a puzzling question. Why kill a good person for someone else's sins?

Visit the author's website: www.donnawelchjones.com